Written
In Ink

Written In Ink

Dream Writer's Chronicles
Book 1

Kelly Dowswell

Kelly Dowswell Books

First Published by Kelly Dowswell Books

Ontario, Canada

@Kelly.Dowswell

Copyright © 2023 Kelly Dowswell

Book cover design moorbooksdesign.com

Paperback ISBN: 978-1-7386699-2-9

Ebook ISBN: 978-1-7386699-3-6

To my husband and my two sons
I love you to the moon and back

One

Cara McDonald grabbed the brown-bagged lunch and gave her cat's head a scratch as she walked out the door. She pulled her fall jacket a bit closer around her neck. There was a nip in the air and could smell the chilly weather coming. Snow would be here soon. Summer passed far too quickly. With the move from her hometown and settling in, there wasn't much time left to relax.

She closed the door, locked it, and turned back one more time to make sure it was truly locked.

Mike and Stephanie, her mom and dad, were already at work. Mike was a doctor, whose practice was now so busy with cold and flu season that he started earlier than usual. Stephanie was a journalist, always busy searching for the next big story. Lately that had meant skulking around abandoned, or partially built buildings, trying to catch a photo of the copper thieves stripping the pipes. Each morning, her mom left in the middle of the night and would come home exhausted while Cara was at school.

She hated that they moved. But the night that Cara's grandmother called because she had had a stroke, her family knew they had to do something. Dad had sat them all down and they decided they needed to move in with her. Only a month later, the home that she had lived in for most of her life was packed up and they were on their way. They each had their own way of dealing with the transition, but the new schedule was lonely.

Cara trudged along the sidewalk, dreading the day ahead of her. Keeping up with old friends was a struggle, and making new ones even after a few months at the new school, was even worse.

There were things she did like about the new neighbourhood though. Thick towering maple and oak trees lined the streets and protected the bungalows tucked behind winding driveways. Each one looked straight out of a 70s magazine and Cara loved it.

She turned a corner and saw the school, peaking over some of the smaller trees on the street. Her steps shortened. As she turned into the parking lot, the towering school, with its three floors, cast shadows over her. She crossed the lawn and ran her hand across the red bricks. Tracing the 1921 plaque, she wondered if kids a hundred years ago hated this building as much as she did.

As Cara pulled open the large wooden door, panic swept over her. She didn't want to go in. But she grabbed the metal handle, rolled her shoulders back and pulled. It wouldn't be that bad, she told herself. She had to be hopeful, for her parents' sake, it had to be okay.

Two

Cara walked tentatively through the wide hall. She pushed past a group talking in the middle of it and headed towards what was still called the photography darkroom. She needed to look over some of the recent weekend photos. Along with a few other students, she was creating a photo insert for the yearbook with a focus on capturing candid and quiet moments instead of staged ones.

Almost at the darkroom, Cara had to dart around another mid-hall gathering. She hoped that in a school of over two thousand students, she would just blend in. Unfortunately, she had caught someone's eye, and it wasn't a good thing. Melissa and her group of friends had spotted her and since that first day, they hadn't stopped harassing her.

That first day of school, Cara had been so nervous, but genuinely excited. She had walked to school with her head held high and by the end of the day had even made a friend.

The girl who's locker beside her had said hi, given her a wink and a smile as she slammed the locker shut before walking away. It wasn't much, but it helped calm her nerves.

The next time they saw each other was after lunch.

"Name's Grace," she said, giving Cara a nod as she packed up the next set of books into her backpack.

"Cara," she replied.

"You're new," Grace said, sizing her up. She gave her another smile, turned, and leaned against her closed locker.

"Yeah, I, uh, just moved here," she said. She took a deep breath and slowly let it out.

"Obviously not used to a place this big."

"No."

"Well, if you need anyone to show you around, I can help with that. I know this town better than I know myself, which makes sense since I'm only seventeen. Lots of time to figure that out," Grace stated.

"That would be really great. I keep getting lost," Cara said. She gave a hesitant laugh and finished switching her books.

"No problem. We'll plan something for the weekend."

Cara felt her shoulders relax. She walked down the hall with what she knew was a goofy look on her face, but she didn't care.

But as she walked down the hall, she felt the hairs on the back of her neck stand on end. She knows now it was Melissa, but on that day, the look this unknown girl with her jet black hair and even darker eyes, gave her chills up and down her spine. It had hit her like a radar gun as she walked past her down the hall. She glanced back to her as she turned into her classroom and saw the girl staring at her. She tried to shake off the uncomfortable feeling she was having but it didn't work.

The next day, she saw Melissa again, only this time, she was with someone else. The tough-looking girl was towering, with fiery red hair. They were both watching her. Melissa whispered something to the fiery girl, who then walked away. Melissa watched Cara until she was out of sight and the girl walked away.

The following day, the fiery girl approached Cara, asking if she wanted to go on a date with some guy Cara had never met. Cara declined awkwardly, but after every class this girl appeared, like out of thin air, and asked again and again. At the end of the day, she asked one last time. Cara shouted no, but the guy was standing behind Melissa, a mortified look washed over his face.

Cara knew she wasn't the most gorgeous girl in the world, but she wasn't ugly by any means. The pigmentless patches on her face may be unusual, but in her own eyes it was beautiful, like impressionist art. She was only seven years old when her mother noticed the white patches starting to appear on her left arm. Her dad took one look and knew instantly what it was: vitiligo, a skin condition that causes your skin to lose its pigment and turns pure white. Her case of it wasn't severe, but it didn't stop the teasing and jokes from coming.

The next day, with her arms full of books and about to leave the school, she was hip-checked by the same fiery girl into a locker, sending her books flying. Cara looked up to see a group of girls around her.

The week after that, the same group walked by and this time Melissa slapped her books out of her hands and onto the floor. Every day it only got worse. One day it was jokes about her not having her Dalmatian coat with her, to not getting enough sunlight and being called Dracula. For a week, all the girls in the group wore garlic necklaces in the halls and made big shows of going around her in a wide circle. Eventually, the girls got more students on their side, and Cara couldn't take it anymore.

"Come in," the guidance counsellor, Ms. Graham, said as she put away a file. "What can I help you with?"

Cara took a seat in front of the small desk. Ms. Graham was a slender woman with a small frame. Even the small desk she sat behind seemed to dwarf her in size.

"You're new here, aren't you?" Ms. Graham said, sitting back in her seat and folding her hands together.

"I started this fall."

"Well, hopefully I can be of some assistance."

"I'm having some trouble with some bullies," Cara said, picking at her cuticle on her thumb. "Melissa and her friends." The first few words felt caught in her throat, but soon they came tumbling out of her. When she finally finished, she looked back at Ms. Graham and waited. Ms. Graham was unreadable.

Ms. Graham sucked in her cheeks and scrunched her nose a little.

"In all the years I've known her, this is the first time I'm hearing about issues with Melissa. I'm sorry to hear this though. I'll see what I can do."

Ms. Graham stood, and Cara followed suit.

I guess we're done, Cara thought as the counsellor led her to the door.

* * *

It had been nearly a week since Cara's last encounter. Maybe talking to the counsellor had helped. She made her way to her locker, switched her books and zipped up her bag. She put it on and spun. Melissa was right behind her, her face only inches from her own.

"Boo," Melissa said with a deep growl in her voice.

Cara jumped and went to run, but she wasn't fast enough.

The fiery girl came up to her and shoved her into her locker, knocking the wind out of her. She fell to the floor, gasping for air.

The fiery girl then grabbed her by the front of her shirt and pulled Cara back up. The girl looked at Cara for a moment. Cara stared back with pleading eyes, hoping for compassion. Unfortunately, she wasn't.

It came like a sledgehammer. The punch to her stomach crumpled her instantly and she hit the floor. Her head bounced off the yellowed tiles and sent a ringing sensation through her head.

A crowd gathered, but no one tried to stop it. Grace glanced at her and turned away. No one wanted to get involved. Cara tried to find one person that would help her, but the pain was too much. She shut her eyes.

The fiery girl moved towards her like she was going to do more, but Melissa came over and shoved her out of the way.

"That is for telling on us. And this is to keep your mouth shut," she said, crouching in front of her for a moment. She flicked her nose then walked away. "Don't cross me again."

The Hammer, as Cara now referred to the fiery girl glanced down at Cara with an evil look in her eyes. She faked another kick, making Cara flinch, then laughed and jogged to catch up with Melissa.

Cara lay curled up on the floor, the coolness numbing her. She slowly rolled onto her hands and knees and pulled herself up using the locker.

Hands shaking, she carefully picked up her books one at a time and put them back into her locker. She wouldn't be able to carry them now. The bell rang loudly overhead and she flinched from the loud sound. She was late for class, which would mean going to the office for a late slip again. She walked into the bathroom and into a stall. The smell of urine and disinfectant made her nostrils burn. She lifted her shirt. The side of her stomach was red and already starting to bruise. She gently put her shirt down and walked out of the stall towards the sink. Turning it on, she cupped her hands underneath, letting the water fill them. She splashed her face, her hands shaking so badly water trickled down her arms. She stopped at her locker again for paper and pen before heading to the office. On the way, she quickly forged a note from her parents and handed it to the office administrator. Cara watched as the lady inspected it, gave her a funny look, but then shrugged before writing a hall pass. She slowly made her way to her class. No one said anything as she handed the note to the teacher and gingerly took her seat near the back.

She watched a couple of students near the front turn back to her and smirk in a way that confirmed they had seen the whole thing. Cara felt heat rising in her again. They had been there and done nothing. They stood there, watched, then walked away like nothing happened. Cara looked down at her notes, hoping her hanging hair would hide the tears that threatened to spill out. She had no idea what was taught the rest of that period. All she knew was that she'd never felt so alone.

Three

The slapping of Cara's flip-flops echoed against the speck-led cement floor. Her breaths were ragged and her throat ached for water. Beads of sweat streamed down her face and into her eyes. She wiped it away, but it still stung. Her heart was racing as she turned down another hall. She didn't know where she was, but she had to keep going, otherwise Melissa and her group would catch up to her. She held her bruised side and ran. Her steps felt slow and sluggish.

Another hall.

The old grey paint made everything look the same. She was so lost.

Left turn, then right.

Cara had avoided her locker that next day. The idea of Melissa or anyone else touching her again made her cringe, but they'd followed her after class.

Another turn, another hall. But now the number of students was dwindling. She was so disoriented. She glanced over her shoulder but still couldn't see Melissa.

The thin group of students behind her moved aside so the Hammer could pass through.

Cara turned again. A dead end.

She spun. Only one door.

She grabbed it and heaved. It stuck.

Leaning back as far as she could, she pulled with all her weight behind her. Panic swept over her. The Hammer was getting closer. Cara pulled over and over again. She looked down. Why wouldn't it move? Then she realized – push.

Pushing it gave way easily, and she fell to the floor, wincing in pain. Cara scrambled to her feet and ran in, slamming the door shut behind her. She was stunned to see the school's pool. She had heard rumours of it, but it was supposed to be out of commission; however, here it was, full of crystal clean water. The next moment, the Hammer burst through the door. Cara turned to run, her thin sandals sliding like jelly along the smooth tiles, but her feet slipped out from under her. She flailed for a moment before hitting the cold water.

Cara looked up through the water and saw the Hammer waiting at the edge of the pool. Surfacing for air, the Hammer grabbed a handful of Cara's hair.

Cara kicked and struggled, gasping and clawing at the Hammer's hands, until she slipped free. Taking a deep breath, Cara dove again, deeper into the water. Her heavy clothing made it difficult to move as she pushed towards the far edge. She looked ahead, knowing she would need more air, and noticed something dark near the bottom of the pool. At first it looked small, but as she swam towards it, she saw it was a tunnel, big enough she could easily fit in it. Maybe it would take her to another room where she'd be safe. Pushing off the bottom, she surfaced, filling her lungs.

"You can't tread water all day," the Hammer taunted.

Cara took a deep breath and dove towards the tunnel and slipped into it. It led her under the pool's edge and beyond. She pushed through, and the light from the room behind slowly faded the further she went. Her lungs ached as the tunnel dragged on. Her vision blurred and darkness was creeping in on the sides.

Was this leading to anything? Cara wondered. She needed air. Closing her eyes, she pushed on, knowing she had already swam past the point of no return.

She opened her eyes again and as her sight cleared, she saw a light streamed overhead. She wondered if it was the light to heaven or to fresh air, but at this point she didn't care. Kicking hard, she felt the pressure changing around her and, with her last ounce of hope, she pushed herself up and burst through the surface of the water. She coughed and sputtered as her lungs burned from the fresh air.

To her right, she saw the edge of the water and a shore-line with soft sand. It wasn't far. Her feet made contact with the ground and she clumsily sloshed to the shoreline and collapsed.

Four

She lay there on the sun bleached sand, eyes closed, and focused on her breathing. It came ragged and irregular at first. As her body calmed, she noticed it no longer smelled like chlorine from the pool. Instead, she could smell mud and fish. There was a freshness to it that the school definitely didn't have. The grit of sand stung her cheek as she brushed it away. She slowly opened her eyes to take in her surroundings. Still on her stomach, she turned her head slightly to look at the water and saw it was a brilliantly blue lake. Sunlight danced like sparkling diamonds on the surface as the wind blew over her.

She gingerly pushed herself upright on shaky arms, looking around, trying to figure out where she was. On the far side of the lake was a cobblestone bridge crossing at the narrowest part of the lake. From there, it turned into a winding river that ran through the open field surrounding it and into the forest beyond.

Movement caught her eye. She turned to see a golden retriever at first, but as she looked past him, she saw there were animals of all kinds. Cara was confused. There were squirrels, monkeys, parrots, and even a pair of lions. She scurried back and gasped after catching sight of a bear, but they all kept their distance. A few of the smaller ones inched closer, and she heard them whispering amongst themselves, gesturing towards her.

They spoke in quiet tones, but she could have sworn she heard one word more than the rest: 'human.'

"Where am I?" Cara asked, getting to her feet. She shook her head. The lack of oxygen must have caused her thinking to be off.

Cautiously, a golden retriever stepped forward, one paw in front of the other, eyes fixed on hers as he approached. His fur shone brightly against the afternoon light, his tail wagging.

"You're a human," he said, looking her over.

She jumped back and stumbled, falling on her butt. She tried to push herself away, but her muscles screamed out in pain.

"This is incredible!" he spoke again. He reached out his one paw, but quickly pulled it back as if afraid.

"I have to be dreaming," Cara said. "Or dead. Oh crap. Am I dead? I drowned in that damn tunnel!"

The retriever laughed, and a few of the animals near him smiled.

"No, you're not dead. You're very much alive. I just can't believe this," he said, barely above a whisper. "This is… This… human!" he stammered at the other animals that were now inching closer. He did a little jump and circled around her.

Every furry face looked back at Cara, just as perplexed, but with a dash of excitement. A wave of goosebumps spread across her body. How were these animals able to talk, and why was seeing a human so unusual?

Before she could answer, the ground started to rumble around her. The eyes in front of her widened as they looked over her head into the distance. A chill spread through her as she turned around to see what they were looking at.

At first, it looked like a mountain, but mountains didn't move. Then the mountain let out a roar that shook the ground under them again. It was an enormous beast, gaining speed and distance fast. His teeth shone brightly against his dark brown fur and he towered higher than the trees of the forest that he crushed without a second thought. The group around her erupted into chaos. The retriever grabbed her hand and ran, pulling her.

They raced through the forest, branches slapping at Cara's bare arms. She stumbled across the uneven ground, the weight of her soaked pants holding her back. Finally, the retriever stopped in front of a tree and knocked on the bottom of it, where the roots indented inwards. A hole opened up, and he wiggled his way down, motioning for her to follow. Cara followed him, and burst through the hole, into a long dirt tunnel. She winced, but there was no time to stop.

The tunnel was well lit with wall sconces, allowing them to see as they made their way through. He led her toward a large wooden door. It had a curved top and a worn copper handle. The retriever opened it and moved aside, letting her enter first, before closing it behind him.

The room was unlike anything she had ever seen before. Despite being underground, the ceiling appeared impossibly high. Floor-to-ceiling burgundy drapes covered the walls, accentuated with gold paisley designs. Golden tassels hung at the sides of the curtains, ready to hold them open when needed. The floor was packed down flat and in the middle was a large rug that covered a good portion of it. Several long tables extended from one end of the room to the other. They were covered in large dust cloths, covering odd-looking shapes underneath.

"Where are we? What is this room?"

"Who are you?" asked the retriever, sizing her up like Melissa always did, but this felt different.

Cara could see his nose moving as he took in her scent. He appeared friendly enough, but so had Melissa that first time she had met her.

"I asked first. Where are we?"

"Maybe so, but how? How did you get here? You're human," he said, circling her. His gaze made her uncomfortable. Ever since she'd moved, she felt as though she was constantly under a microscope. She could feel the heat rising in her again. How dare he gawk at her like this?

"I honestly don't know. The last thing I remember is the Hammer chasing me. There was a pool, and I fell in. You said I'm not dead, so I have to be dreaming, right? She actually got me out of the pool and knocked me out?" Cara crossed her arms, hugging herself, and shifted her weight from one foot to the other.

"A hammer was chasing you?"

"No–it's–never mind."

"Well, you're definitely not dead."

"So, will you please tell me where I am? And who are you?"

He came closer to her, his tail wagged back and forth, his golden fur shimmered in a smooth line. Cara paused for a moment but then slowly felt herself calm.

"Of course. The name's James, and you are definitely not dreaming. Not right now, anyway."

Cara squeezed a few drops of lake water out of her shirt and onto the floor. "I don't understand."

"Let me try to explain. This, my dear," he said, motioning towards the room, "is the Room of Dreams."

Five

"The what?" Cara asked, looking around her.

"The Room of Dreams," James said, looking around. She watched as he walked over to one of the dust sheets and, with a sparkle in his eye and a flourish of the wrist, he pulled it off, revealing rows upon rows of typewriters from Smith-Coronas to Underwoods and Imperials.

She gasped, then walked over to the nearest table. She had always loved these classic typewriters, and this one was probably the nicest she had ever seen.

She let her fingers run over the casing of a Smith-Corona. It reminded her of the one her grandmother always had on the tidy desk in her office. Every time Cara visited, she could hear her hitting the keys with a matchless fury. She could watch her type for several minutes before her grandmother would finally leave the world she had been writing and notice her. She frequently typed with her eyes closed, fingers flying across the keys, hitting them with precision. Cara often tried to get her to switch to a computer, knowing it would be faster and easier to make edits but her grandmother always said no. She loved the feel and sound the typewriter made as it hit the paper with such force that sometimes Cara thought the typebars would snap. After the stroke though, her grandmother couldn't type anymore, and had given the typewriter to Cara, even though she wasn't a writer.

As she looked at the keys of the typewriter before her, she could picture her grandmother there. The black casing shone brightly against the overhead light and the keys twinkled as though ready to go to work.

James had stopped talking and she could feel his eyes watching her, enjoying her reaction. She crossed her arms again and looked at him, eyebrows raised.

"So, what exactly is that supposed to mean? 'Room of Dreams,'" she asked. She walked back to the doorway and waited for some form of explanation.

"Well, whether it is the dreams at night while you are sleeping, daydreams, or the dreams of what you want to accomplish in this life of yours, it is all written here on these typewriters."

"That doesn't make sense. My imagination writes the dreams."

"That's what most people think. But they don't know about us. In reality, the dreams are written here on these typewriters for every human to experience."

"Then somehow we get the dream? As if," she scoffed.

"Exactly," he said, walking over to one typewriter and adjusting the stack of paper beside it.

"You seriously expect me to believe this?" Cara asked. She walked over to the table again and took a long look at a 1940s Corona typewriter. She could tell it was well used, but taken care of. The casing had minor scratches, but it looked like someone had recently polished it. The black paint shone so brightly that Cara could make out her reflection in it.

"Well, it's the truth," he said, bringing her back to reality.

Cara looked at him again, watching him walk around the typewriters and stopping every so often to clean off a smudge of dirt from one of them. She thought she must be dreaming all of this.

"So you write the dreams, we get them and... that's it?"

"Well, there's more to it than just that, but that's the main part of it."

Cara picked up a piece of paper sitting beside a typewriter. It was thick and pale ivory in colour, like cardstock. How was she expected to believe there was anything different about it? She set it back down and walked towards James. If everything he was saying was true, then they must write not only the good dreams that woke her up with a smile on her face, but also the nightmares that left her in a cold sweat.

"If you write all the dreams, that means you write all our nightmares too, then, huh?"

James turned on his heel and quickly busied himself with pulling the rest of the dust sheets off.

"Yes. It's the side of the job we don't like, but we have no choice."

Cara watched as he balled up the sheets and quickly put them away. She tried to look into his eyes, to see what he was thinking, but he refused to look at her.

"Who's we? And why do you have to write them? Why not just make everyone have good dreams?" she asked, following close behind him.

"It is not for us to decide what dreams you have. We only write them." He pulled the last sheet off and rolled it into a ball before tucking it into a cabinet near the doorway.

"There are multitudes of us. We take turns writing, plus there are other rooms." He looked at the clock on the wall above the boxes, his eyes sparkling even in this low light. "You'll see."

Suddenly, the room shook violently. Everything rattled on the tables and across the floor. Two crystal candle holders fell off a nearby table and shattered onto the floor.

"What's going on?" she cried.

"It's him! Hurry! Get to the doorway. I think he might have followed us."

The rattling continued for a few minutes and Cara watched as the once clean typewriters were now covered in a layer of dirt that fell from the ceiling. Finally, when it stopped, Cara crept out of her hiding spot under a table. James stood and sighed. He grabbed a duster in the same cabinet and started walking around dusting the typewriters off.

"What is going on?" she said, attempting to brush the fallen dust off her damp shirt.

James looked at her, turned and headed over to a near-by doorway.

Cara watched him go, and after a moment, he returned with a handful of clothes.

"I do not know how well they'll fit, but try these on. You can't stay in wet clothes. You can change just in there," he said, pointing to a bathroom nearby.

"Thanks."

Cara took the clothes to the room and slowly changed. This had to all be a weird dream she was having. She had never heard anything like this before and there was certainly no way a bunch of animals were able to write dreams, was there? She slipped the dry clothes on and was shocked to find they fit. In fact, they almost fit too well. She wasn't sure what this place was, but every question James answered only brought more to mind.

Six

"So, can you at least answer my question?" she said upon returning. She looked at him and tried to size him up, but that wasn't so easy. How do you read the body language of a dog?

"It's not so simple," James said. "You won't understand."

"Try me."

He motioned for her to take a seat at one of the typewriters and sat next to her. He kept his gaze down, wringing his paws until finally he put them down and looked up.

"Years ago, a woman came here from another land. I suspect yours. She was so sweet and lovely initially, but something happened. She let in a darkness that wasn't here before. And ever since, we've had that — that thing roaming around here. It terrorizes us. It makes sure we write the dreams. Some have tried fighting it, but anyone who has tried has failed. They haven't come back."

"They didn't come back? Do you mean they died?"

"That, or they are being held somewhere. We don't know, but either way, we haven't seen or heard from them since. And we stopped sending out search parties because it's just too dangerous. We can't chance anyone else not coming back." James rubbed his head for a moment, clearly upset.

Cara stood again, pacing the room.

What have I stumbled upon here? She thought, looking back at this talking dog.

"So wait, the beast ensures you write the nightmares? But who actually makes you write them?" She stopped pacing and walked over to him.

"The woman, Sarith does. She sends them. Then the beast makes sure it happens. He's her muscles, so to speak.

"Obviously, we don't enjoy writing the nightmares. We always try to write them before the good ones. That way, everyone who has those terrible things go through their minds is at least left with something positive before they wake up. They are more likely to remember the good ones and less of the bad ones."

"How does the beast know if you have written them?"

"A copy gets sent back to Sarith. Once we tried not writing them. The dreams after that were only worse. We couldn't sleep for months. They were violent, terrifying. It was worse than we had ever expected. All the dreams written here and in the other dream-writing rooms and halls are all brought here. From there, I have to send them."

"You know how nuts this all sounds, right? Animals writing dreams for humans and beasts of anger and darkness doing the dirty work for some power-hungry woman?" She looked at him doubtfully.

"It's the truth."

Cara turned to look at him and could see the frustration in his eyes. She returned to him and took a seat.

"So, how exactly do you send the dreams? Let me guess, carrier pigeon?" Cara sat back as a chuckle escaped her lips.

"I know you don't believe me and even if I told you how it's sent, you still probably won't believe me," James said.

"Probably not, but go ahead."

"Well, it's magic."

"Right, magic," she said, crossing her arms again.

"This is a pretty magical place, actually. When we write the dreams, it's on enchanted paper. As soon as it's finished, it becomes a person's dream. Afterwards, the supervisors bring the paper here and it goes into the enchanted boxes that the beast leaves for us." James walked over to a table on the far side of the room and on it sat five large wooden boxes with bronze buckles. He opened one, showing it was empty.

"When I place it in here and close the lid, the paper disappears and reappears in her palace. If she's content, we don't hear anymore about it. If not, the beast comes for us." He closed the lid and leaned on the large table.

"Okay, so who is this 'we' you are talking about? I don't see anyone here but us, and there's no way you do all the dreams on your own. There are too many people in my world," she said.

Just then, a very subtle rumble started again, but this time Cara could hear it through the walls of the room. The curtains swayed and, one by one, they opened up and revealed dozens of creatures pouring into the room. There was everything from squirrels and rabbits all the way to miniature hippos and baby giraffes.

Eventually, the room was full and the rumbling ceased as everyone got to their seats, waiting for that day's stack of dreams.

Cara stumbled back as she moved aside. All around were animals of every size, shape and kind, and they were all getting along. Lions and lambs were cracking jokes together while the cats were playfully wrestling with the dogs. Every creature was so unaware that in another world, they were supposed to be enemies.

"These are my fellow writers," he said, extending his paw out to showcase them.

"All of you? You all get along and write the dreams?"

They looked at her and most either smiled or waved. She could tell they were happy to see a human in their world, but most tried to keep themselves composed. A few of the younger ones, like the baby giraffe, let her head bob around, clearly excited.

"We do get along. And, as for the dreams, for many years, the dreams we got to write were great. We had the chance to show people their true heart's desire. We have always been told what to write, but we could write it in a way we knew would ring true with them. And we could tell those dreams not only inspired people but showed them anything was possible. As the years went on, we saw people following their dreams and making their lives into what they always wanted. They were taking chances and believing in themselves. They were taking risks and, with each one, there were substantial rewards that were only getting better every day. Even we found it rewarding. We got to sense the joy people got from the good dreams. The worlds were such happier places as people did what they loved.

"But Sarith made the beast appear," James said, his voice breaking slightly.

"Was she the first human to come into this world?" Cara asked.

"Yes. She was." As he spoke, a loud bell chimed from somewhere in the room. "That means the dreams are ready."

From behind James, a large chocolate-brown moose emerged, walked past her, and to the entrance. He disappeared down the hall. She chuckled. She couldn't help herself. How was this reality? A moose? James leaned over.

"His name is Brownie."

"Of course it is," she said, rubbing her forehead.

Brownie re-entered the room and on his back was a large box, like the ones James had shown her.

James went with Brownie to a distant table and opened the box after Brownie placed it there. Inside were handwritten pages. James slowly distributed them to the animals around the room. As each animal looked at their stack, she could see anguish on their faces. They were reading the dreams they would be typing and sending to the humans, just like her. Her breath quickened as she remembered some of the terrible dreams she had had. Many times she would wake up in a cold sweat and her heart racing.

"Listen, I know what nightmares are like, even the night terrors. I've had many. You can't write these. You just can't." Cara ran up to the first animal she came to, grabbed the stack of handwritten pages, and gripped them close to her chest.

"Cara, we don't have a choice," James said.

"But you can't! You don't know what kind of anguish this causes people. You have to stop, you have to!" She ran over to the boxes Brownie placed on the far tables and slapped the lids down. The sound echoed in the room and made some writers jump. Cara went to the next writer and grabbed their stack and the next one, and held as many as she could in her arms. She tried to carry them all, but they spilled all over the floor. She readjusted and tried to get the next stack, but more fell. James approached her and tried to take them back.

"We have to do it. It's worse, much worse," he said, emphasizing the words, "if we don't write them." She looked into his eyes and saw compassion, but also pity. She knew no matter how many stacks she tried to take away, she was powerless to stop them. There were too many and, if James was telling the truth, this was only one of many rooms, which would mean her efforts were point-less anyway.

Reluctantly, she gave back the papers to him, and he led her to a small kitchen. He motioned for her to get herself a glass of water. She watched him for a moment as he re-joined his fellow writers and redistributed the papers. Then, without a word, he walked back to her and leaned on the counter. There was only a moment of quiet before she heard the typewriters coming to life. The snapping of the keys echoed into the kitchen and made her head spin. It was nearly deafening. She covered her ears, but it barely made a difference.

James motioned to the kitchen table. On it was a set of headphones with a microphone attachment. She slid them on and instantly felt some relief.

"There's a volume dial on the left ear," James's voice said through the earpiece. She adjusted accordingly.

Each animal sat at a typewriter, their paws moving with precision over the keys. Pages filled and every so often one of them would pull the sheet out and the next would be put in. The stacks of typed dreams grew before her eyes.

Cara felt her heart race. Anxiety washed over her. A hot prickly sensation slowly crept up the back of her neck and into her hair. It spread into her ears, the tips of them burn-ing fiercely before travelling down into her jaw and to the front of her neck and chest. Even knowing she was power-less, she still wanted to rip the paper out of all the type-writers, run away, and destroy it all. She watched James walk around and stopped every so often to put his paw on a shoulder. Then she understood what his job actually was. It wasn't to supervise to make sure they wrote the dreams; it was comfort them. He'd see them shiver or have tears run down their faces as the words they typed shook them to the core. She could only imagine how horrible the words had to be if they caused this kind of reaction. And that's when her own thoughts quieted enough that she could finally hear it. Over the crashing of the typewriter keys, the faint sound of James's voice came through her headset in murmurs. He was whispering words of comfort to the writers as he stood beside them, trying to make the task easier.

What felt like hours passed before the mood of the room shifted drastically. Relief washed over their faces. They must have moved on to the good dreams. James took a seat at an empty typewriter and typed fast but with precision. After a while, the room became quiet again and everyone sat back in their chairs and a collective sigh rang out around the room. Cara took off the headphones.

"We did some good work tonight, everyone. Have a good night."

As the room emptied, Cara made her way over to James. Exhaustion washed over her, even though she hadn't been through the emotion they had.

"Time for sleep," he said.

He led her to a small bedroom off of the main room. The main centrepiece was a large mahogany fourposter bed. Rich, thick velvet hung down from them in sweeping shapes. She immediately wanted to disappear into the thick feather duvet that laid on it. Opposite the bed was a small table and two chairs, perfect for a cup of tea or a spot to read.

Cara looked back at James after taking in the room's beauty and finally let herself relax.

"You've been pretty nice to me, even though I'm just a stranger," she said.

He shook his head. "You might be a stranger in one sense, but we know you. We wrote your dreams."

"I guess that means you know me a lot better than I realize," she said, suddenly feeling so exposed.

James motioned for her to have a seat at the table, and he took the other chair.

"You asked me to explain. And if you aren't too tired, I'd like to take the time to answer at least a few more questions."

Cara motioned for him to continue.

"Well, first, this is my home. I have lived here pretty much all my life. Because of this, I'm the supervisor of the typewriters. My father and the generations before that passed my job down to me. It has been my family's tradition since the typewriters first began. It's an important job and one I don't take lightly. Most of the time it isn't difficult to do, but sometimes it comes with its challenges. I watch the typists at night. I must always make sure no one tries to write anything unauthorized," he said. He sat back and stretched out his tense muscles.

"Does it happen very often that someone will sneak in and write something?" she asked.

"Not very often, but sometimes. There is a group of writers that come in during the day and write the daydreams for everyone. There is a supervisor for that one too. Although still important, daydreams don't need as much supervision, so I could let someone else take over that portion. That way, I could get some sleep and do some everyday things too."

All of this, as baffling as it sounded, also made so much sense. But something still nagged at her. She just couldn't shake it. She straightened herself and picked at her nails.

"James, I have to know. Why was everyone so stunned to see me? Was it just because I'm human?"

"Cara, you are the second human ever to enter our world. That's a pretty big thing for us. We have often wondered if another human would enter our land. We always hoped, but we never really expected it." James let out an enormous yawn and stretched.

"But for now, I must be off to sleep. Sleep tight." He turned and left, pulling the door behind him. Cara watched him go, then turned to the room. The light from the many burning candles he had lit, filled it with a warm glow. Shadows danced across the cream walls and something about it was so comforting.

She quietly made her way around the room and slowly blew out the candles. Wisps of smoke waltzed up from the extinguished flames. As she crawled into bed, the painting above it caught her eye. It was an open field filled with tall, wild grasses. There were two trees, one on either side of the painting's edge, that grew towards the middle. Multiple branches intertwined and gradually covered over the field, making them almost look like braids. She turned away, but quickly did a double take. She could have sworn those branches were moving.

"Now I know I'm tired. Things in paintings don't move."

She made herself look away and pulled the sheets up high. Her eyes were already heavy with sleep and even though this place was so foreign to her, she drifted into a dreamless sleep.

Seven

Cara woke the next morning to rapping on her door. She quickly made her way to it to find James holding a tray of food. The smell of it immediately made her stomach jump and hunger overtook.

She held the door open and let him pass, and he took it over to the table.

She sat and he placed the tray in front of her. He had made up a full plate of fluffy pancakes drenched in maple syrup, muffins, toast, and a glass of orange juice.

"If you need anything, please don't be afraid to ask," he said, turning to leave. Cara watched him walk to the doorway, his shoulders slightly hunched.

"Hey," she said, and he turned. She rubbed the back of her neck and looked down at the plate in front of her.

"Have you eaten anything yet?"

"I have not. I have some in the other room though."

"Well, there is another chair here if you want to, I dunno, join me." There really was more food than she would ever eat. Her appetite had dwindled since moving.

He tilted his head and held up his paw before slipping out of the room, only to return a few moments later with another tray full of food. "We'll have quite the feast, won't we?" he exclaimed, sitting down and motioning for her to start.

They sat together, the stillness between them almost thick.

What do you say to a dog? Cara wondered, watching him. He didn't eat the way dogs typically do. It was very similar to humans, in fact. He used a fork and knife like she did. It struck her as odd. But why should it? Everything else in this world seemed strange so far, so why not eat with a fork and knife?

He took a giant bite of toast and wiped his lips. He looked down at his lap again.

"Everything okay?" he said, politely covering his mouth with his paw as he asked.

Cara put her fork down and leaned back in her chair. She had stopped eating and was just watching him. He had obviously noticed.

"I guess so. It's just a lot to take in right now."

"I understand. And it might take some time to really take it all in," he said, setting his fork down and sitting back.

Cara took a sip of juice. How much time was he expecting? What was he really excited about here? There was definitely something else, but he wasn't telling her just yet.

"Well, this has been kind of interesting to learn about, but..." she said, but continued the thought in her head. She really should think about finding her way home. As much as they had been nice to her and saved her, she really just wanted to get back to her parents and home. They would be so worried about her. She never stayed overnight somewhere without at least calling first.

"Wait until you see the town!" James interrupted, taking another big bite of toast. "It's absolutely incredible. The homes are all handmade and it's nestled against this gorgeous mountain. It's really something to see. And so many will want to meet you," he said, pushing the toast into his cheek to talk.

Cara took another nibble of pancakes. It sounded like the type of place she would like. She always loved the rustic and homemade places back at home. Maybe it wouldn't hurt to humour him on this, even if it was just to see what they did. But realistically, she couldn't stay. Just one quick walk around the town and then she would mention going home.

They finished up and Cara helped James take everything to the kitchen.

"James, where did the beast come from? You said she made it appear, but what does that mean?"

James put the dishes down in the sink with a loud clank and took a deep breath. He slowly turned towards her, but refused to meet her gaze.

"How about I tell you on the way? We have a ten-minute walk, anyway."

"Sure."

James led the way out of the dream-writing room and into the tunnels.

The tunnels were disorienting, just like the school halls. They twisted and turned and she tried to mark each turn, remember every tunnel, but eventually gave up. It was all dirt walls, dirt ceiling, and torches jutting out from the hardened mud, and everything smelled like earth. They wandered around, seemingly in circles, before James finally led her up an incline and found themselves on grass as soft as felt. All around her, trees rose impossibly high, towering over them and giving an umbrella of shade. The uneven ground was covered in leaves and undergrowth.

As they walked, they came up to a fallen tree that had split open on contact and was now teeming with insects. Whispering reached her ears as she stepped over it. The sound was coming from the log. She stopped and bent over it and even though they were quite tiny, one word could be heard again and again: "human."

She shook her head. How silly she felt. Her mind must be playing tricks on her. She jogged to catch up with James, who was now further down the path.

Birds called overhead and crickets sang as they walked. She took a deep breath and the cool, misty air felt good in her lungs. Waves of calm passed over her. Even at home, when she went for walks, she never felt this peaceful, yet somehow it was different here.

Then she remembered the beast and how it had snapped trees this size to trying to get them while they were at the lake.

"The beast, do we need to worry about it around here?" She asked with a shaky voice.

"If we did, then we wouldn't be above ground," James said, shooting her a sly smile.

"Are you sure?"

James nodded.

"You were going to tell me where the beast came from?" Cara asked.

"Yes, well, it came from that woman Sarith as far as we know. I'm not exactly sure about all the details.

"After she came, everything seemed to change. A darkness came into this world and the beast appeared. It didn't seem too bad at first. We actually thought it was a new animal that came to this world to live in peace like we have for so long, but it quickly showed us it wasn't friendly at all."

"How did it do that?" Cara asked.

"Well, when it was first found, it was only a fraction of the size it is now. I tried to be friends with it when I first met it and it was okay. It let me hold and carry it around. I didn't know what animal species it was, but I welcomed it anyway, like we've always done in our community. But as it grew, its mood and energy changed. I could see the aggression rising in it. Eventually, it bit someone. Then it began destroying things and attacking others. No one died, but some were seriously hurt. At this point, it was getting very large, and we decided as a town to move it along to somewhere else. But before we could, it was with Sarith and getting bigger by the day. We feared the worst, braced for it even. Then she started using him to terrorize us. And she's only getting more and more power happy and angrier. I think he's a manifestation of her anger that's taken on this beast's form."

"That can happen?"

"It's the only thing that makes sense. When we're happy, we can make new animals appear. We can create, build, and do just about anything that makes us or our world better. With her being a part of such darkness, what if she could use it to create things that hurt, destroy, or even could kill us?"

"Why don't you just destroy it?" Cara asked.

"We aren't strong enough and definitely not strong enough to defeat her. Her magic is stronger than all of us together. Humans seem to have stronger magic."

Cara stopped and looked at him again.

"And I'm human," she said. Now she understood why he didn't want her to go. Being human, he would expect her to have stronger magic than they had. And if that was the case, they would expect her to do something about Sarith.

"Yes, but don't worry about it. You are our guest," James said.

"Let's be real for a moment. Someone is going to expect something of me."

"Possibly, but please don't worry about that. Just come and see the town. It's so lovely."

She looked around, lost in thought. She just wanted to get home and now they wanted her to save their lives? They knew nothing about her and what she could or couldn't do. If they really knew her, they wouldn't even dream of asking her to do this.

"Look…" she said, wanting to tell him the truth, but her voice trailed off as she finally looked up and saw the town. She didn't want to admit it, but it really was beautiful. Just like he said, it was nestled against the snow-topped mountain. Warm points of light in the town went out one by one as the town awoke. Fireflies drifted back towards the mountain to find places to rest for the day.

They entered through a large wooden gate and passed two guards, who looked at her curiously. The walkway opened to a large courtyard with five cobblestone streets branching out from it. Large oak and maple trees lined them, giving flickering shade. The air was fresh, just like after a spring rain.

Cara looked around wide-eyed. It almost looked like a town from one of her fairytale books she had as a child. She opened her mouth but nothing came out.

James laughed.

"I told you that you'd like it."

Eight

He led her down one of the narrow streets off the centre court and deeper into town. The smell of fresh baked goods from a nearby bakery greeted them as they walked. The homes and businesses huddled close together, creating a cozy feeling. Many of the homeowners peeked their heads out of their windows, watching and talking amongst themselves as Cara and James walked past. She knew they were talking about her.

"You'll have to forgive them. They haven't seen too many humans before," he said, chuckling.

"Yeah, I'm noticing. Who's place are we going to again?" she said awkwardly, trying to change the subject.

"We're going to my good friend Woodrow's home. I've known him for as long as I can remember. He's the one person who I trust to help me take care of the Room of Dreams when I need a break or I'm sick. I think you'll like him."

They arrived at a small home near the middle of town. It was fairly modest compared to the surrounding ones.

Large stones of muted colours made up the walls. Each looked like it was placed there one at a time and held in place by thick ash-coloured clay.

James knocked on the large wooden door and immediately it opened. A grey squirrel moved aside, allowing them to enter. His grey tail with a white tip flicked this way and that, while his nose twitched. Cara noticed his paws were white marbled like her own skin.

"You're here! Come in! Come in!" he said, barely able to stand still. Cara entered first, while James hung back. She didn't even have to look back to know they were exchanging an excited look.

"This is incredible!" Woodrow said, barely above a whisper.

"I barely slept last night. It doesn't seem real!" James whispered back, then they followed her inside.

They had entered a spacious room, with the kitchen to the left by a window overlooking the road. The dining room was in the middle, separating the kitchen from the living room on the far right. Three doors branched off it to bedrooms and a bathroom.

"Sit, sit! I just put the kettle on," Woodrow said, darting over to the kitchen.

James chose a spot on the couch in the living room. Cara followed and chose a plush chair across from it. All of this sat in front of the home's main fireplace. The large stonework ran around the fireplace's open hearth and continued up the wall. There were two wooden shelves partway up the wall, both with simple drawings by someone young.

A small vase with some dried flowers and a candle finished filling the shelves.

"What are your plans today? Are you two just taking in the town or are you planning to do something else?" Woodrow asked, his paws fidgeting.

"Well, I want to show her around and meet some of the townsfolk. The art gallery has that big exhibit opening this afternoon, so I thought I would take her to that. Most of the predominant folks should be there." James said.

Woodrow sat down, but then got up again. He beamed. Cara caught the look in James's eye, too. They were both trying so hard to hide their thoughts, but they were doing a terrible job at it. She could tell James wanted her to save them from this beast and this woman, but how could she even think about doing something like that? It was impossible. Especially for a nobody like her. But how would she tell them that? Maybe she would get lucky and they wouldn't actually ask and she could just go home, assuming that was an option. She couldn't let them expect her to save them.

She would go along with this tour of the town and be shown around, but in the end, she would find her way home.

Nine

Sarith pulled her hair back and wove it into a loose braid and shook out her shoulders. She felt the tension slowly release as she eyed the boxes in front of her. The highly polished wood shone against the bright morning light that filtered through the nearby window. Here, at the top of the east tower of her castle, she had set up her own dream room.

The outside walls were lined with tables that had boxes resting on top. In the middle of the room was her desk. It was a deep mahogany table with stacks of notebooks ready to be filled.

This was her favourite part of the day. The moments of quiet when she could gather her thoughts and plan her day. She picked up one of the thick ivory paper sheets the dreams were typed on and could already see the words forming on it. The nightmares she would have the animals write would send shivers up their spines and have them reeling. She let the paper fall back into the box, picked up a notebook, and sat down. Her pen stood poised on the paper. Closing her eyes, she took a deep breath and let the pen go to work. She wrote quickly and quietly, feeling wave after wave of goosebumps going down her spine. She loved that feeling. It made her feel so alive.

Quickly, page after page filled. She stopped and opened her eyes. She looked back at the pages, now curled at the edges from the pressure she had used to write them and smirked.

When she first entered this world, all she had hoped for was to go home. But after spending some time with these creatures and seeing how well they had treated her, she had changed her mind. This world saw her as more than just the unsuccessful person she was. She had always thought she was destined for something special, but years of disappointments and things not going the way she expected showed her different. But here she had power and it had been intoxicating. She had never felt so strong.

She thought about home once in a while. At some point, she had completely lost track of how long it had been since she had seen her husband and daughter. But at least the girl was a teenager now. She would be mostly self-sufficient at this point. Sarith wondered if they missed her, but she shook off that thought and pulled her shoulders back. She was sure they wouldn't. Sarith had a temper she never managed to control, even on her good days. And the last argument with her daughter had been especially bad.

Sarith put the pen down and shook out her hand. All this time, and she still was getting wicked hand cramps from writing for too long.

The window flew open, slapping against the stone frame. Sarith jumped and held her chest.

"What is the meaning of this?" she demanded, throwing the book down and going to the window.

The beast stood back from the window and waited. He was now too large to enter the castle, but would come to the windows to be given his orders.

"I need you to come with me," he said.

"You know this is my time to get the dreams ready!" she scolded.

"This is important."

"What could possibly be so important?" she said, walking back over to the table and picking up the notebook. She brushed it off and reopened it to the last page.

"Another human."

Sarith stopped and looked at him. The notebook fell out of her hand to the floor.

"Excuse me?" she managed to say.

"You need to see this."

Sarith grabbed her jacket, threw it around her shoulders and took a step towards the window. She doubled back for a moment, grabbed the book, and put her hand above it. She watched as the pages filled with words. They turned slowly at first, but soon were flipping fast. Once complete, she closed the cover. She knew magic was faster to write these dreams, but it wasn't as satisfying as handwriting. Something about a pen on paper was so much more fulfilling and more real.

She ran over to the window and swung her legs out. Pushing off the ledge, she landed hard on the beast's back.

She grabbed a handful of fur and kicked her heels in. The beast took off.

If he was telling the truth, then maybe she would finally have someone to challenge her. Lately, she had grown so restless. Now might be the time. The idea both excited and terrified her.

Ten

The beast took her to the lake, and upon arriving, Sarith knew something was different. The beast showed her the footprints and said the one word that made her shudder: 'human.'

She slid off the beast, knelt down, and looked at the mess of prints. Many she recognized from her time here, but one set stood out amongst the rest; one she hadn't seen in this land. It was human. Her skin erupted in goose-bumps as her fingers gently touched the treaded print. Even in this thick mud, she knew this woman was wearing sneakers, something she hadn't seen in years. They remained in one area, then took off towards the forest and were lost in the grasses.

"Impossible!" Sarith yelled, looking at the beast in front of her. She pushed her long, black hair off her shoulders and turned towards the lake. Normally, this clear body would be teaming with life, but not now. The presence of the beast was always enough to send them off in fear.

She slowly stood and rubbed her fingers together, feeling the mud drying and crumpling. The beast beside her grew restless and let out a bellow, shaking the ground around them and sending vibrations through her chest. She flicked the mud off her fingers and spun towards him, grabbing his thick mane and tugging it hard and pulling his face pulled close to hers.

"Enough!" she hissed, and he immediately silenced.

"It's true," he growled at her. "I saw a woman. A human."

"Tell me everything," she said, before pushing him away. The beast stumbled slightly before getting his footing. He shook himself all over as though he was trying to rid his coat of water.

"She didn't look to be all that old," he said, deep growls quivering in the background of his voice. As he walked, the ground vibrated, sending dandelion seeds dancing across the grass. Not even the birds dared to fly overhead.

Sarith paced back and forth as the beast spoke.

"She came in right over there," the beast said, motioning towards the lake.

It had been a long time since she had come here. The longer she stayed in this world, the more she forgot about her life back home. The memories were becoming more like clouds being blown away in the wind. But as she looked at the lake, the day she had come into this world came back to her like a movie playing in her mind.

It was a rainy day and the raindrops bounced off the lake like flies off a bug-zapping light. Sarith got herself to shore and once she had caught her breath, she had wandered around the woods for days before she had finally found anyone. The first time she heard an animal speak had filled her with such fear, she had run back to the lake. But she couldn't bring herself to go back to the real world to face all the responsibilities and disappointments.

So, she stayed. As time went on, she met the townsfolk and what was now her beast. And everyday she found more reasons to stay. The last time she came to the lake, she had planned to fill in the tunnel. She knew she would never leave, but something stopped her from doing it. She had a nagging feeling that someday she may need to go home. So, she left it as was, but relocated all the fish, bringing in new ones that didn't know about the tunnel. And unless they knew where to look, it wasn't easy to find.

"I didn't see who led her away," the beast said. "They were too quick."

"Oh really? Or is it just that you are getting too soft? Their speed should be no issue."

The beast let out a growl again, this time throwing its head back and arms out.

"Enough!" she screamed, but the beast only growled louder. She walked over to it and grabbed its mane and pulled hard, bringing its head down to her. "Enough," she hissed.

"What do we do now?" He huffed, clearly embarrassed to be scolded in such a way.

"We find her. And we destroy her," Sarith said, pushing his head away. She turned and walked back towards her castle.

"How?"

"By any means necessary."

Eleven

"Listen, promise you'll come back at some point and say hi again!" Woodrow said as Cara and James stood to leave.

She gave him a stiff wave and followed James out the door.

"Sorry, I know Woodrow can get a bit… excited? Is that the right word?" James asked, as they walked through his yard and closed the small wooden fence surrounding his yard. He stopped at the road and smoothed down his hair. He brushed his arms off and rounded his shoulders, gathering himself together before turning right down the street.

"That's one way to put it, I guess," she said.

"Anyway, let's go introduce you to a few folks," he said, a twinkle in his eye.

* * *

Cara and James walked along the main street, Cara's shoes tapping slightly against the cobblestone. The large picture windows of the passing shops boasted of everything from sweet treats to books to young ones laughing over toys at a toy shop. With each shop they passed, James would give the slightest nod, head held high and golden fur ruffling in the wind. When they acknowledged him back, he added a little trot to his step. Cara could tell he enjoyed the attention.

They turned down a small side street and James stopped in front of the largest window she had seen and turned to face her.

"Ready?" he asked, his face lit up with excitement.

Before she could answer, he grabbed her hand and led her inside. The entryway opened to a large foyer. The ceiling rose high in the middle, with the above floors surrounding the opening. Animals stood against the railings, looking down towards them, some waving at her and James.

He led her away to the right, where the main exhibit started. Tables with champagne glasses and food trays ready to be loaded up with snacks were tucked in the corners of the room. Wait staff were bringing out decorations and setting up tables for folks to rest their drinks on.

"We're early, but that won't be an issue."

Each room was filled with the same type of medium: charcoal in one, watercolour in the next, and so on.

The first room had metal sculptures, but they didn't enter it. Instead, they went to the second room that was filled with acrylic paintings. Cara paused in front of one.

The colours felt real, like they were flying off the canvas and grabbing her soul.

"We have some very talented artists in this world," James said, smiling at Cara's reaction.

They made their way around the room, taking in each piece, some for longer than others.

Cara stopped in front of a painting of wildflowers. They were in a field with a small waterfall flowing in the background, but Cara barely reacted even to the actual water that moved in the painting. James knew this was an unusual piece, even for their world. But Cara just moved on. James paused a moment before watching her walk away. Finally, he noticed the slumped shoulders, the slow walk, and the grey clouds that hung over her.

"What's going on?" he said, catching up to her.

"These are nice," she said, moving along to the next piece.

"If they are just nice to you, then you really aren't seeing them," he said, shooting her a look.

Cara looked up at him and back at the painting.

"What are you talking about?" She looked again, confused.

"This piece has moving water in it!" He poked his finger into the water and showed her his wet paw. Water splashed onto the floor and she jumped back to avoid it.

"Oh!" she managed, before walking back in front of it and taking a better look. She slowly lifted her hand up and put her finger into the water. It was cool and refreshing. It dribbled down her arm and onto the floor. She pulled away and wiped off what she could.

Silence fell over them as she shifted slightly, and took a step towards the next piece, but then pulled back.

"Is there something wrong?" he asked, watching her and not sure how to proceed.

She just shook her head and finally made herself move to the next piece.

Wrong? That didn't even begin to describe how she felt right now. In fact, nothing was right. She was in a world full of animals, looking at art, hoping to bide her time so she could get home and away from all this craziness. But honestly, what was at home for her? A bully ready to make her life a living hell. That idea didn't sound much better, but at least she wouldn't be terrorized by the beast and a woman she assumed would try to kill her if she saw her as a threat. How could she tell him that, though? She barely knew him. The last time she had shared something with people she barely knew, they had turned it back against her.

"I'm just fine," she stated flatly before taking a step towards the next painting.

Silence hung in the air like a thick blanket of fog.

James wrung his paws as he stood beside her.

The silence broke as a pair of foxes came in, their laughter echoing in the empty room.

"Oh, excuse me!" one of them said, when they saw James and Cara. They stopped and even from the other side of the room, Cara could tell they didn't know what to do.

Before she could say anything, James walked towards them, his face set. His shoulders hunched down and his expression completely changed.

"Gentlemen, you're here early," he said in a flat tone.

"We wanted to make sure everything was just right for the show. You know how detailed Michael can be," said the other one, winking at Cara.

"And you guys are...?" Cara said, looking back and forth between the pair.

"Where are our manners? I'm Anthony," said the first one, "and this is my brother Michael," he continued with a bit of a flourish as he turned towards his brother. "We are part of the city council with James here."

The two were nearly identical, and Cara was having a hard time telling them apart as they circled and paced around each other. Both had copper-coloured fur with white faces. But Michael's white patch on his nose was in the shape of a heart, whereas Anthony's was more like a star. Michael had bright blue eyes and Anthony had one blue and one brown one.

Being the youngest out of the council, sometimes they struggled to stay focused, but the others always kept them on their toes. Most folks, upon meeting them, often expected to be liars or at least tricksters, as many foxes are, but they weren't.

"Oh, you're on the town council? That, along with the Dream Writing, must keep you pretty busy," Cara said, turning to size James up.

"I am," James answered, but turned back to the twins.

"Would you mind if we join you both for a walk around the gallery?" Michael said.

"That's up to Cara," James asked, clearly trying to be polite, but she could see the irritation in his eyes.

"Sure, why not? The more the merrier," Cara said shrugging, trying to sound happy about it, but knowing it was coming out flat.

"So this painting over here is…" Anthony said to James, pointing to the next piece.

The twins led them all over the gallery, pointing out the best pieces.

Cara couldn't believe there was so much talent in this world. Not that she didn't think animals were capable of doing some amazing things, but this was so different from what she had ever expected. The twins pointed out sculptures that seemed to almost float in midair, and paintings that moved with no help. The colours were unlike anything Cara had ever seen before. Somehow, they seemed brighter and bolder than any of the ones at home.

"You seen this one before?" Anthony asked, pointing to a picture of the small fishing boat amid a large storm. The water was moving even now and the dark, threatening storm clouds swirled overhead.

"Can't say I have," James replied, leaning in a bit to get a closer look through squinted eyes.

Cara and Michael walked up behind them and Cara leaned in, too.

"My buddy John and I were making it years ago. It was at his place because he was finishing it up. Anyway, he got so fed up with it that he took it from the easel and tossed it on the couch. He couldn't get the storm clouds just right, so he goes into the kitchen to make himself a cup of tea and, of course, that's when I show up. I've got movies and snacks. I knew he was having a rough time with this piece, so I came to surprise him and hopefully distract him too.

"Well, I walk in, my arms are totally full of stuff and I can barely make out where I'm headed. I head over to the couch to sit and put the snacks on the table and just as I'm making contact, I hear him cry out. I didn't know I was about to sit on the painting. Next thing I know, the snacks and movies go flying and I'm falling through the air and then 'splash!'"

"You fell into the painting?" James said, trying to keep calm, but snorted with laughter.

"Yep! I had to swim for my life just to get out of the water and into the boat. Thankfully, that fisherman was in there to help me out of the water or I would have been a goner!"

"Wait, you... you fell into the painting? How is that possible?" Cara stepped right up to it and looked it over. "You can't fall into a painting!"

"You want to try it out?" He laughed. "Personally, I don't recommend it. I was scared for my life! I thought I would die in there!"

"But that's impossible!" Cara couldn't see how that could happen; yet the fisherman in the painting looked at her and waved his tiny hand. She slowly waved back, stunned.

"You don't know the half of it," Michael said, agreeing.

"You won't believe how calm that fisherman was, but I guess he's probably gotten used to the storm by the time I fell in there! Me? I was terrified!"

"How did you get out?" Cara asked.

"How else? John reached into the painting and pulled me out!"

James, Anthony, and Michael all laughed together, leaving Cara feeling like she had missed the punchline.

"Why were you scared when you fell in then, if you knew he could reach in and save you?"

"Well, he couldn't exactly find me when I was in the water, could he? And those waves are so high. Look at how dark it is! That storm is a lot scarier when you're in it than what it looks like from the outside.

"Anyway, I had to get to the boat. Once he saw me there, he had no problem."

"Why doesn't he help the fisherman, then?"

"Because his job is to fish," Anthony replied.

They laughed again and he slapped Cara on the back. "You have so much to learn about our world."

"I guess so," she said, gently shrugging him off. She might have a lot to learn, but she wouldn't be here long enough to know for sure.

"We still have some time, so how about we get some lunch before everyone else comes. I know I'm hungry and we can show her the rest later."

They walked out of the gallery and down the street, heading towards the bakery she had seen earlier.

"They have the best scones you have ever had," Michael told Cara as they walked. James and Anthony walked ahead.

"I do like scones." She paused. "Michael? Your brother is a bit more outgoing than you are, isn't he?"

"Oh yeah, but I think that's what makes us a good pair. Life would be boring if we were both the same, wouldn't it?"

"But do you ever feel you're being overshadowed a bit?"

He thought for a few moments before speaking, and when he did, his voice was steady.

"Maybe sometimes, but I know he doesn't mean to. He's just being himself, like I'm myself. I have my time and shine in my own way. He doesn't outshine me all the time." He winked at her as they entered the cafe.

The smell of fresh baked bread wafted over her. She took a deep breath and sighed. Even in this place, far from home, that smell still brought back memories. She and her friends would stop for croissants at the bakery around the corner from the school. They always got croissants and ate them outside on a small patch of grass beside the bakery. They would spread butter over it and let the sun melt it deep into the bread before taking big bites. The sweetness of the bun and the salty butter was always the perfect mix. Her new school had nothing close to it. And even if it did, the friend situation wasn't good.

On the other side of the room, a few arms flew up and waved them over. At the table was a lion and a rabbit.

"Hey! What are you all doing here?" Michael asked.

Cara stopped short. She had never been so close to a lion. Even though she suspected he was friendly, she was terrified. She had seen what a lion could do to someone back in her world.

"Don't worry," the lion said, "I'm friendly." He gave her a big toothy grin that just reminded her how he could tear her to shreds if he really wanted. She sank into her seat, but tried to keep some distance.

"I'm Terrance," he said, holding out his paw for her to shake. She leaned closer and hesitantly shook it. It was huge and dwarfed her hand. No one back home would ever believe she shook a lion's paw.

"So, Cara, what do you think of our little world so far?" Anthony asked after they ordered teas and croissants for the whole table.

"I haven't seen much of it yet, but so far it seems... lovely," she said, whispering the last word.

"We think so too," Cynthia, the white rabbit with bright blue eyes, agreed. "Tell us about your home."

"Honestly, I haven't really lived there all that long. I don't know much about it."

But the little she did, she hated it. The city was huge and loud. Everywhere they went felt congested and as though there was no room to actually breathe. Litter lined the major streets. Only their subdivision seemed quiet.

"Then tell us about your last home. What was it like?" Anthony said, sitting up as the server came over with their drinks.

"Well, it was..." Her voice trailed off slightly, her mind searching for the right word. She thought of the beautiful nature trail on the outskirts of town. The path led out of town and to her favourite wooden bench near a small pond. Many times, her best friend would meet her there and they would sit, brainstorming ideas for where to go exploring for their next batch of photos.

"It was home," she stated. "I left my best friend, Ryan, there with the promise I would continue to write to him and send photos of my new place. Only, finding beauty there is much harder than I expected."

"You are a photographer!" Terrance said, taking a drink.

"Well, I'd like to be, but nothing of mine is in print yet, so, not technically a photographer yet."

"The moment you hold the camera up to your eye, line up the shot, and hit the shutter, you are a photographer. You have created something. I would love to see what you could do with a camera in a world like ours."

"Um, yeah, I guess," she said, looking down at her hands. Since they said goodbye, Cara refused to even think about Ryan. She hadn't written him since she moved, and the stack of unopened letters from him sat waiting on her desk. She knew she would have to open them at some point and reply, but being at this new school, in this new town, was more difficult than she had planned for. And if she was truly honest with herself, she was embarrassed that she was being bullied so much. She didn't think she could reply to him and still seem like the happy person he had known her to be.

"Tell us more!" They all agreed.

Cara took a deep breath. Maybe talking about it would help.

Slowly, the words began. They were forced at first, but once she got going, they flowed out like a river. She found herself telling them all about her past home: how it was small and quaint, how it was welcoming, and how much fun she had there. She told them about walking along the creeks in the area, looking for wildlife, bike rides with Ryan, extra-thick chocolate milkshakes, and adventures that, no matter how much time went by, she never forgot. Saying goodbye to the town she grew up in was the hardest thing she had ever done.

She told them about the day the phone call came. Her mom had answered it and by the end, she was in tears. It was when they found out that Cara's grandmother had had the stroke. They had moved quickly after that. But this new city was cold and unforgiving, or at least, that's the way it felt to Cara. Where her hometown had warm nature trails and beaches, this city had concrete slabs and towering buildings that reflected the chilly winds in harsh ways. Her trails were now roads, with cars speeding past in hurried attempts at getting to the next meeting or appointment on time.

She missed the slower pace of her hometown, but it seemed no one understood it. She had never felt so alone in her life, and each time the bullies taunted her, it only reinforced her feelings.

Cara felt the tears welling up in her eyes, but tried to blink them away. She had never let anyone see her get this upset since she moved, and she wasn't about to start. She coughed loudly, trying to clear her throat.

Anthony looked down into his coffee, obviously unsure how to deal with her emotions. At that moment, the barista came over and broke the silence that had fallen on them by letting Michael and Anthony know they had a call.

They excused themselves, while Terrance and James turned to discuss something.

Cara took a couple of deep breaths and felt her heart beat going back to normal. When she finally looked up, Cynthia turned to her and gave her a warm look.

"Sounds like home is very different from here," Cynthia said.

Cara laughed, taking a big drink of tea.

"You have no idea."

"I want you to know you are not alone. If you need a friend, I'm here. I might not know exactly what you're going through, but I am good at listening."

Cara turned to her and looked her in the eye. She instantly felt the walls coming back up around her.

She remembered the last time she had someone say that to her. It was the Hammer that first day of school in the girls' bathroom, before she really knew her. They talked and Cara quickly found herself telling this girl things she didn't expect to tell anyone about this early in a friendship. There was something about her that made Cara feel like she could really trust her. Cara opened up about how scared she was in a new school and how she really didn't feel like she belonged. It had been a rough week. She had tried to extend the hand of kindness and friendship to several girls in her class, but no one seemed to want to reciprocate. That girl in the bathroom was the only person who had been kind to her. She had been a caring, listening ear on that island of loneliness and fear. The girl had given her a hug when Cara finally broke down crying. It had been so nice to have someone to talk to that she didn't even notice they weren't alone, until suddenly a laugh rose up from one of the stalls. Melissa walked out, cell phone raised above her head, the entire conversation being replayed for her. Cara was confused. Why would someone record that? Why would anyone care?

Then she heard her voice saying how lonely she was and how sad she was on the recording. Cara felt her cheeks immediately go red with embarrassment and she ran out, crying as she ran through the halls to her locker. She tried to hide her face as she grabbed her backpack and headed to the door, but some students still saw and snickered and whispered. Some even pointed at her and giggled to themselves. She wanted to disappear.

She barely slept all weekend. What would these girls do with the recording? What was the point of it? When would they fire back with it and use it against her? She talked herself down enough to get herself back to school.

When the morning announcements started Monday morning, she instantly recognized her voice over the speaker system. The recording Melissa had was playing for the entire school to hear. She was mortified, and didn't know what to do. She could hear her own sobs, not just through the speaker system, but she had started too. The class whispered, some laughing, before the tears blurred her vision and she ran into the hall. She heard a teacher cut Melissa off and try to apologize, but it was too late; the damage had been done.

It took weeks before her classmates stopped taunting her and coming up to her, mockingly reciting the conversation for her again and again. Even though that was two months ago, she still wasn't over it. Would she ever truly be? She knew it would stick with her for the rest of her life. Her parents tried for weeks to find out what had happened, but she never told them. She just couldn't.

"That's what they all say, but then when you least expect it, they stab you in the back," Cara said, coming back to the present moment. "Forget this. I'm out of here."

"But there's so much left to see!" Cynthia said, looking confused.

"I'm done. I'm leaving."

Cara walked out, leaving Cynthia speechless.

Twelve

Cara burst through the front doors of the cafe and looked around. Her vision blurred behind a veil of tears that threatened to unleash. She swallowed the lump forming in her throat and gave her head a shake. In front of her, the town passed by, but she could barely notice it. She began walking but didn't know where to go, only that she had to get out of there. She took a few deep breaths but they came out ragged.

But as she wandered, and her tears stopped, she saw the animals were turning and looking at her, but it wasn't because of her tears. Each one that locked eyes with her, showed only hope. She knew she couldn't save them, and for them to hope otherwise was ridiculous.

She knew walking out on Cynthia had been rude, but she had been burned too many times. Every time she thought she was past it, something would set her off and this time was no different. Even though home wouldn't be much better, she had to try and get back. At least there, she could disappear into her room and pretend everything was fine. Sure, it would be terrible to know that this world was being terrorized by the beast and all the bad dreams would be because she hadn't stopped him from taking over, but she couldn't do anything about it. And the sooner she could get home, the sooner they would forget these crazy hopes and maybe just move on.

She wandered through the city square and past the incredible water fountain in the centre. The sunshine glistened in the water as it flowed down the different levels. Cara stopped to watch as streams rose up from the pool at the bottom and twisted their way back up to the top, before descending again. The mist fell gently on her face, washing away her tears. She took a few deep breaths before wiping her face with the back of her hand.

"Cara?" She caught sight of James standing before her, watching her. She didn't know how long he had been there, probably just long enough, though. She let herself fall on the edge of the fountain. Her shoulders fell forward and she rested her head in her hands.

"What happened? Why did you take off?" He sat down beside her and looked out towards the rest of the square.

"I just, I couldn't do it."

James looked at her with a mix of understanding and sadness and slowly nodded his head.

"When someone's hurting it can be really difficult to see anything as just the simple, sweet gesture that it's supposed to be."

"How could you possibly..." She didn't know how he knew that, but maybe she was just that easy to read. Regardless, waves of exhaustion flowed over her and suddenly all she wanted to do was go to sleep.

"Come with me," he said, walking ahead of her. She was reluctant at first, but finally she caught up to him and followed. Where they were going she didn't know, but at least getting out of the main street would mean she wouldn't have to see the crowd from the cafe for a bit and for that, she was grateful.

Thirteen

Sarith stormed into her castle, her shoes echoing on the cold stone and her dress flowing around her. She entered the main meeting room, opening the doors wide as though the room was breathing in, then let them slam shut behind her. In the centre of the room was a square table with tall chairs all around. Normally this would be where she would meet with the general of her ever-growing army, but today she passed through and headed out towards the back. That's where General Barabus held his daily training sessions with the troops.

As she entered the courtyard, the cool air from the neighbouring mountains made her skin erupt in goose-bumps but she barely noticed. Before her stood her army. They currently had three-hundred troops and every day they were hunting for more. Recruiting wasn't easy, though. Most didn't want to join, but General Barabus was very persuasive, both with this strength and his looks. Being a black gorilla with broad shoulders and a muscular upper body, most of the animals were intimidated by him.

Sarith stopped and watched as the troops climbed walls; crawled in the obstacle course they had created; and lifted heavy weights. She could see the strain on their faces and the deep breaths of steam coming from them as they worked out. They would be ready no matter what came.

She paused only a moment before the General saw her and rushed over.

"Ma'am? Everything okay?" he asked, a concerned look washing over his face. She never came out here, and she knew her presence unnerved him.

"General, we must speak. In private," Sarith said.

He led her away to the far end of the yard. It was quieter here, yet they could still watch the troops.

"It's time, General," she said, straightening her dress. "Another human has been spotted in our world. A woman."

His eyes snapped back to her after having looked away to the army for a moment.

"A human? But how?" he asked.

"That doesn't matter. Right now, what does is locating her and bringing her here. We cannot have her attempting to disrupt our lives."

"What's the plan?" He straightened up and waited, ready for the order.

Respect, she thought, watching him. She loved it.

"I want you to gather the army up and we will attack by nightfall. That should be more than doable, correct?"

"Today?" he gulped, clenching his fists.

"Is there an issue? Because there better not be," she said, her eyes blazing. She could feel her anger rising. Nothing made her angrier than when things didn't go her way. Anything less than perfection was unacceptable.

"Well, no, there isn't, but…" he let his voice trail off. She knew he was trying to be cautious with his words, which normally she demanded, but not today. There was another human spotted here and she would not rest until that person was apprehended and in her custody. His hesitation was now just annoying and time consuming, and the longer he took to find his words, the higher the heat rose from her neck into her face.

"Spit it out! We don't have all the time in the world here."

"Do we know anything about her? Like if she has magic?" he asked.

"What does that matter? She's no match for me. You think someone that just came into this world is stronger than me?" She scoffed at the very thought of it and watched as the army continued to train. A honey badger caught her eye across the yard. He looked far too small to have any strength, and she knew it was only a matter of time before he would fall. He glanced up at the wall he had to scale. Sarith watched as his shoulders slumped slightly. Taking a deep breath, he made first attempt. Only making it up halfway, he fell back down and bent over, hands on his knees, clearly stopping to take a deep breath. He dragged himself back to his starting point and tried again. This time he almost made it, but was still short.

Sarith shook her head. She could forgive missing once, but twice? And if she didn't stop it now, how many more times? She flicked her wrist and watched as he flew up and over the wall and fell hard behind it. Even at this great distance, she could hear the leg snap. He screeched out in pain and she could see him grabbing at it. She laughed to herself, then noticed General Barabus was watching her and had stopped talking altogether.

"What?" she smirked at him. She crossed her arms over her chest and watched as another couple of animals raced over and helped him up. They carried him away towards the medical area to tend to his leg, but they all knew that a break caused by human magic would take months to heal, if at all.

"Ma'am," he said. He hesitantly met her eye-line again.

"She won't be stronger than me," Sarith said. "I don't see how it's relevant if she has magic or not. Either way, we need to find her, bring her here, and after that, I can deal with her."

"But if she does have magic, not as strong as yours, of course, but if she does, then we need to be prepared. If you defeat another human, especially if she has magic, in front of all of those animals from both sides, think of how much they will fear you! They will be terrified. They will see that you truly are the strongest one here and they won't hesitate anymore to join our side," he said.

Would they really come willingly? she wondered. There was something thrilling about the hunt for those creatures. They were always so difficult to catch and make fight for her, but once they saw the light, her light, they quickly gave in. Or was it because of their extensive force? She never knew, but either way, they always gave up.

What if he was right, though? If she could build up the army with the townsfolk, then she could rule all of this land. They could even start branching out and find more land that she could conquer. There had to be other towns in this world.

Her name would precede her. She would have the largest army anyone had ever had. She could see them already, sweat glistening on their brows as they fought. All for her name. Something about it gave her a warm feeling inside. Power was intoxicating.

"Fine. We won't attack right away," Sarith said. "I want you to find out if she has magic or not. Report back to me once you know. If she does, this victory will be so sweet."

General Barabus nodded and hurried off towards the medical tent, Sarith assumed, to check in on the animal she had injured. She laughed and turned away. Winning a battle against another human would be sweet, but winning one against another human with magic? Well, that would be delicious.

Fourteen

James and Cara rushed along the side streets and back towards the town entrance. The guards looked at them questioningly as they disappeared deep into the forest. Here, the air chilled quickly, being away from the protective walls of the city. Cara shivered, but kept moving.

"Are you taking me back to your place?" she asked. James had wanted her to see the town so desperately, but now their sudden departure stunned her. Even in the confusion, she felt a glimmer of hope starting to burn in her. Maybe he finally understood that she wasn't a hero.

"Not quite," he said, but didn't meet her eyes.

"Then where?"

"You need to go home. I'm going to help you get there," James said, stopping at a massive tree that had fallen on the path, blocking their way. He looked all around it and found a small hole near the bottom that he quickly slipped through to the other side. Even at a distance, Cara knew she would never fit inside. She looked for a way around it and found that to the far left side of the pathway, it seemed to rise slightly, giving her enough height to hoist herself up and over it. She dropped to the moist ground on the other side. The grass underfoot soaked the sides of her running shoes. She sighed, then stepped over a larger puddle before reaching the hard soil. James had stopped down the path, waiting for her to catch up, but she could see the impatience in his eyes.

"But what about the town and the beast and Sarith?" she asked as she caught up with him.

"I've been thinking about this," he said, turning back to the path. "Maybe the lake will still have a way for you to get home." He pointed to her left and they turned, heading away from the mountain.

"Really? But the creatures here," she said, not finishing her sentence. She wasn't too sure at this point if he would even truly hear her anyways.

"I see everything clearly now. It was ridiculous for us to expect anything from you. You'll be much happier at home and I think we shouldn't waste our energy talking about it. We need to get you there before anyone comes looking for us. We left with enough haste that it would have caught someone's eye."

So, Cara let James lead her along the thick undergrowth and back towards the lake. He wasn't sharing it, but she knew he had a plan already. And she wasn't about to argue against any plan that got her home.

James stopped dead in his tracks and held his paw out. He took a step backwards and leaned against a tall oak tree, ears perked. He quickly motioned for her to do the same. Slowly, he turned his head to look around the tree and saw in the distance a figure sitting on an old tree stump. It stood and slowly turned around, like it could sense they were there.

James pulled his head back and looked at Cara, motioning for her to stay still.

He took a few breaths before looking again and saw that the figure was closer, and heading towards them. His eyes remained locked on where they were. James saw the figure's chest sparkle as he turned and James realized it was a chest plate.

"It's General Barabus!" he whispered into Cara's ear. She looked at him confused.

"Sarith's General," he said.

Panic swept over her. They both looked around the tree and General Barabus stopped. James locked eyes with him, then his eyes fell on Cara. A smile crept over his face and he charged.

James grabbed Cara's hand and bolted. They ran as fast as Cara could manage, but General Barabus was gaining on them. Behind her, Cara heard sparks starting to fly and she looked back just as he released something. It looked like a fireball. It hit the ground behind them, sending them flying. They fell to the ground and knocked the wind out of her. The world went silent. She looked and saw James, struggling to get to his feet.

He said something, but it came to her thick and murky as though they were underwater.

She pulled herself up and looked around, confused. The General was only twenty feet behind them. Reality came back into focus. She grabbed James this time and pulled him along, running the way they had come and back towards town.

James pointed up to their left and they turned slightly. Ahead was a rock wall, blocking any way out. Cara tried to say something, but James reached down beside her and knocked on the edge of a rock face. An enormous boulder slid over, revealing the tunnels below and both of them dropped into it and the rock slid shut behind them.

They moved a few steps into the tunnel and stopped. Everything was still too murky to make out as she strained to hear. James pointed overhead and she finally heard General Barabus's footsteps overhead. He was cursing and stomping on the ground. James motioned calmly for her to follow him.

He let his paw trail along the wall, stopped, and reached into the darkness beyond. It came back with a lantern and some matches. He lit it and Cara sighed with relief.

"He doesn't know all the ways into these tunnels. But believe me, he's tried."

"Who was that?" Cara asked as they headed down the tunnel.

"That was General Barabus. He's the general in charge of Sarith's army. Now that he's seen us together, he will assume you're staying with me, which puts you in even more danger. We need to change that. I think we need to move you."

"To where? Can't you just take me home?"

"Do you know how close we were to the lake just now? If we go there, either he'll be there waiting for us alone, or with his army. Either way, I don't want to be a part of that.

"And when we don't show up there, he'll expect to find you with me in the dream-writing room. If that's the case, then he's probably going to try to attack the room just to get to you. We can't have that for so many reasons." James continued down the tunnels, turning this way and that. Cara trailed behind, trying to keep up.

"The only thing that would be even remotely safe right now would be to take you back into town and to Woodrow's house. He won't expect you there.

"In the meantime, I'll have to look into getting more security at the dream-writing room. I can't imagine that he'll destroy the place. It's too important. But he might make it more of a nightmare in other ways."

"James, stop. We need to talk about this. If I just go home, then the threat will be gone."

"And what do we do when he doesn't believe me that you've gone home?" James asked, spinning abruptly to face her. "What then?"

The thought hadn't occurred to her.

"Let me get you to Woodrow's before we do anything else." He turned back the way they were going and pressed on. "I don't think going home will be an option right now."

James knocked on what looked like a wall and a doorway opened. Light streamed in and once her eyes adjusted, she saw they were back at the town entrance.

James turned to the guards, said something in whispered tones, then led her back into town. This isn't what she wanted, but she would have to stay for now.

Fifteen

James and Cara knocked on Woodrow's door but didn't wait for him to answer. They pushed the door open. Woodrow was curled up reading and hadn't noticed them.

He looked up from his book, clearly confused, and stood. He scurried over to them, his fluffy tail hanging low.

"We encountered General Barabus," James said, walking to the cupboard. He reached into the back and found a dusty bottle of rum. He unscrewed the cap and took a large swig. Cara and Woodrow watched, both stunned.

"What happened?" Woodrow asked.

"I was taking Cara back to my place, and we were going through the forest, and there he was. He tried to attack us, but he doesn't know the tunnels well enough to actually follow us. But you can guarantee he thinks she's going to be with me. We need to keep her here, with you, otherwise he's going to attack the dream-writing room and that will be the end of everything."

"Uh, yeah, I guess that would be fine," Woodrow smiled.

"The extra room all set up?" James asked.

"Yes, that's not a concern," Woodrow said, his tail lifting finally.

"Good. I'm heading back to my place to set up some security. I want us to keep an eye on the lake too. Maybe he knows something we don't. For now, you two need to stay inside. I don't want him coming to town and finding you. We have to keep you safe."

"So, where's this room I will stay in?" Cara asked, abruptly.

Woodrow pointed past her and towards a door that led to a small room. She grabbed an apple off the counter and darted inside, closing the door behind her. If she was honest, she didn't want to hear them talking, even though their voices carried through the door. Flopping onto the bed, she closed her eyes. This bed wasn't as comfortable as her own back home. This one had a lump on one side. She pushed herself up and looked at the bed, seeing that the blankets were now a mess. She smoothed them out, then let her eyes drift around the room.

It was pretty simple with a double bed, bedside table with a hard-covered book on it and, on the opposite wall, a plush reading chair. On the wall, to the left of the bed, was a large window with the drapes pulled shut. She threw them open and looked out. It wasn't much of a view, mainly just the neighbour's home, but she could see some animals as they passed by on the street closer to the front of the house. No one seemed aware she was there.

They were so happy and some even seemed to have a bounce in their step. Cara didn't understand how they could be joyful when their chances of being destroyed were so high. Did they even understand?

Closing the curtains, she turned around. She knew James wanted her to do something with the way he had been talking. Yet, she was just some simple high school kid with nothing going for her. She stopped herself. When had she gotten this low? She got back up and wandered around the room before finally settling down on the bed. She picked up the book. It was deep navy blue with gold edging on the pages. Opening the front cover, she quickly got lost in its pages.

It told of how the animals had come to this land after months of searching for a new home. They had heard stories about a land that was free and had the freshest water anyone had ever dreamed of, but no one dared travel to it. It was too far. But their town was running low on resources and rumours spread of deadly predators nearby; hyenas.

Then, one night, the hyenas came and attacked. It was swift and at the end of it the hyenas had driven them out, and taken some of their leaders hostage and killed others. A team tried to rescue the ones taken, but many had come back wounded or near death. The hyenas sent the wounded ones back as a warning to stop trying. Eventually, townsfolk knew it was fruitless and, salvaging what they could, they packed up and moved.

And so, they travelled as far west as they could, towards the land that they had heard about for generations.

They walked for days and the water supplies dwindled. They rationed what they could and saved what they had for the young ones. The parents became weak, knowing they couldn't go on for much longer. Only the hope of what they had heard kept them pressing on.

Then one morning, they decided the next day would be their final and if they died without making it, then at least they had tried. They couldn't go on anymore. Some adults were seeing strange visions of things that weren't really there.

As the day wore on and their sight clouded with hallucinations, the leader pointed a shaky finger towards the horizon and gasped. Everyone thought he too was hallucinating; some just shook their heads as they trudged on, but only moments later, they saw it too. The lake was in front of them. They ran towards it, some falling as they went. They jumped in into the cool water and drank until they felt like they were going to be sick.

"I can't believe we made it," the leader whispered, watching the group of them laughing and splashing in the water.

"This is our home," he said in a loud voice that caused everyone to stop and listen. "This is where we will stay from now on. We won't let anyone drive us out of here," it quoted him saying.

And from that day on, the animals remained here. They had lived a quiet and peaceful life for many generations.

And that's where the book ended. Cara flipped it over and noticed at the bottom it stated that it was the first volume.

Woodrow had knocked at some point while she was reading, but she wasn't sure how long ago that was now.

She opened the door and the main room was dark. Day had turned to night. The clock read midnight. Outside her door was a small plate of food she knew would be cold, but she was too hungry to care. She took it back into her room and quickly devoured it before turning out the light and getting into bed. She knew she should try and save these animals, but the images of Melissa's laugh as the Hammer's fist crushed her skin and bones, sending throbbing pain all throughout her reminded her of how powerless she truly was.

She knew there was nothing she could do. Even if she wanted to help them, she knew she couldn't. She was just a worthless girl. She had nothing to offer. Cara rolled over towards the wall and curled herself up into a ball, holding her knees tight against her chest. She hoped sleep would come quickly.

Sixteen

Cara woke to the smell of faux bacon sizzling on the stove. She rolled onto her back, her eyes still closed and took a few deep breaths. Her dad was probably at the stove, watching the bacon dancing in the simmering grease. He loved cooking breakfast for the family Sunday mornings. Mom would be sitting at the table, drinking a steaming cup of tea, while reading the newspaper.

She smiled before slowly opening her eyes and saw the white popcorn ceiling above her. She looked around and as sleep fell away, she saw she wasn't home. Then, all the memories came rushing back to her. She wasn't in her house. She wasn't even in her world. She was somewhere else. A world filled with animals, dreams, and a beast that terrorized everyone and everything. Her heart sank. She knew she came into this world through the lake, and part of her wondered if she could get back out the same way. But James's words came back to her. What if he was right that the General or someone in his charge was now guarding the lake? She wouldn't be able to get through without being seen.

But maybe, she thought as she got herself dressed, under the veil of night, it would be easier to sneak there and get into the water. The bridge was on the far side. If she could just make her way there, she might have a chance. She could hide behind the posts of the bridge. Plus, she could hide in its shadows.

The idea rolled around in her head before taking hold and she finally felt herself relax. Yes, if she could get to the bridge, maybe she could get herself back home.

She adjusted her shirt, then headed out to the living room.

"Hungry?" Woodrow asked, as he scurried back over to the kitchen.

She didn't really feel like eating but the smell of breakfast was too intoxicating to say no. She saw the dining room table was already set with silverware and a tray with a steaming teapot and two matching cups.

She poured herself a cup of tea as Woodrow turned away and pulled pans out, placing them on the stove. He grabbed his cup and walked over to the teapot and poured himself a cup as well, his small paws just fitting around it.

Out of the corner of her eye, she saw the cupboard door move. Cara rubbed her eyes. It was only her and Woodrow here and he was by her and the table. She chuckled to herself. Clearly, she was still tired. Cara looked back and the door was closed, only now two plates were on the counter. They hadn't been there before. Shaking her head, she pinched her arm. She jumped and watched as the blood rose to the surface of her skin, making it red. She was definitely awake.

"How do you like your eggs?" Woodrow asked, walking to the fridge and pulling out a carton of eggs. She opened her mouth to speak, then the words got caught in mid-air. She watched him open it and two eggs lifted out by themselves and floated over towards the frying pan. A knife with some butter tapped against the pan and, as it hit the hot surface, the butter sizzling. The eggs still hung in the air as if waiting for instruction.

"Cara?"

She turned to him and stared. Her mouth hung open.

"Oh yes, sorry. I guess this isn't easing you in, but my cooking needs magic to be edible. Trust me. I think the butter is going to brown in a moment."

"Scrambled," she whispered.

The eggs knocked against the counter before breaking open and into the warm pan. Woodrow ground a little salt and pepper into it. He stepped back as a spoon came over and mixed them together. Cara watched them fluff up. Woodrow rushed over to pour the eggs onto a plate and slid it over to her.

He chuckled at the stunned look on her face. "It's pretty amazing, huh?"

Cara took a bite of the eggs. They were perfect. She took a long sip of tea and dove into her breakfast. Then, when she finished, she sat back in her chair. She took another drink of tea, which was still piping hot a half hour later, but somehow that had escaped her. Woodrow took one final drink and gathered his plates. She hadn't noticed that he had already eaten.

"Let me at least help you with the cleanup," she commented, picking up her dish and holding her hand out for his.

"Oh, don't worry about that. I've got it."

His plate lifted up and floated over to the sink, which had just begun to fill with water. A glass bottle of soap tilted and drizzled in while they were talking. Bubbles rose into the air. The plate in her hands pulled itself free and slid into the soapy water, while a wooden brush scrubbed it clean. A moment later, it was out again and onto the drying rack.

"Yeah, we don't really do dishes here. We figure there are more important things that we could do with our time," Woodrow shrugged.

Cara laughed and shook her head.

"And this is just a normal day for you?" she asked.

"Yes, I guess so. I was thinking I could get your help with some gardening this morning until James gets here. I think from there we will try to show you a few things. Maybe even a bit more magic."

"Alright," she said with little conviction. She would go along with it for the time being, but she would try to sneak away to the lake the first chance she could.

* * *

James returned to Woodrow's home and found the two of them in the small backyard gardening. He watched for a moment while Woodrow showed her how to press the dirt around a plant and make sure it was firmly in place. Woodrow loved his gardens and they rarely were lacking in care or beauty.

He let out a whisper of a sound and Woodrow's ears perked up. Woodrow glanced around and spotted his friend near the back of the yard, near an opening in the fence that Woodrow had refused to close up. He loved letting the garden creatures be able to come and go as they pleased. It always made the plants flourish that much more, he claimed.

"Aren't you going to come over?" he asked, as he reached James. He looked at Cara who still hadn't noticed they were talking.

"Can't. After running into General Barabus, I'm not letting myself go very far. I think I might need to put some lookouts around the lake too. I wanted to tell you I probably won't be around much today. But I want you to take care of Cara for me, if your schedule allows."

"I have nothing planned," Woodrow replied.

"I want you to do another thing for me," James said. "I want you to find out if she has magic, or maybe she can figure out how to have some magic."

"I haven't seen anything yet," Woodrow said.

"Even still, there might be something there. We just need to try. We must know for certain before we can do anything to her."

Woodrow finally looked at him.

"Do to her? What would we do to Cara?"

"I meant to Sarith, of course," he stammered. "Show her what you do," he continued on. "Show her some tricks in the garden. Maybe that will intrigue her. But don't do too much all at once. We don't want to scare her off."

"I did use it to make breakfast. You know what my culinary skills are like," Woodrow laughed. "Wouldn't it be wonderful if she does have magic? Do you know what that could mean for us?" Woodrow bounced up and down.

"Don't get your hopes up just yet. She may not have any magic at all and if she doesn't, then you and anyone else that hopes she does will be disappointed."

"That's true," he said.

"Listen, I have to go, but let me know how it goes and if you find out if she has magic or not, okay?"

Woodrow agreed and watched his friend leave. He returned to Cara and saw her planting more tiger lilies along the house.

"See? Doesn't that look better?" she asked. He noticed not only that she planted the flowers, but the area was now bordered by large stones that his neighbours had left on the property line.

"They won't mind me using these, right?" she asked.

"Not at all. They told me I could use them if I wanted."

Cara picked up the empty watering can.

"Where's the hose? These will need a bit of a drink before I can say I'm actually done."

"We don't need one."

She looked back at him questioningly and caught a glimpse of sunlight dancing off the water in the can.

Cara jumped back. The can fell from her hand and spilled all over the grass. Her mouth dropped open, but no sound came out.

Woodrow bent over and picked up the can. "Sorry, it's easy to forget you're not used to this."

"It's okay," she said, stammering. "It's just been a lot to take in." She took a deep breath and pulled herself together.

"I understand. Maybe we should do something else for a bit. Would you like to go to the farmer's market with me this morning? We can get some fresh ingredients for dinner tonight."

Cara shrugged and followed Woodrow. She turned back and looked over at the garden they had created. With his hand raised, he snapped his fingers. Water sprayed over it. She thought it was a sprinkler, but then she saw them: small frogs that had been in the pond at the back of his yard had made their way over. Using their mouths, they carried water and showered the flowers. They were making a big loop from pond to garden, drenching each flower with water. She laughed lightly.

Woodrow grinned to himself. It was going to be fun to show her everything.

Seventeen

Woodrow led Cara down the street to the town square. All around the perimeter, merchants set up tables filled with everything from fruits and vegetables to jewelry and artwork. They slowly made their way around as Woodrow picked up the things he needed for his meals for the week. Every table said hi to them both, most trying to not stare at Cara, but she could feel the gazes that lingered just a little too long. She tried to busy herself looking at the items on the tables, but no matter what she did, it felt awkward and she just wanted to move on.

"Sorry about, well, everyone," Woodrow whispered to Cara as they left Milly's Produce stand.

"I guess I understand, but honestly, it's making me uncomfortable."

"I think I'm just about ready to go anyway," he said, offering her some understanding.

Woodrow stopped once more before finally saying his goodbyes and leading Cara back towards his home. Woodrow, and his use of magic, made lunch. They had salad with fresh blackberries, feta, and various vegetables, some of which she had never seen before, all drizzled with a vinaigrette dressing. For dessert, Cara watched as he took the fresh cream they had bought and he chilled it and churned it into fresh ice cream, all by magic, and topped it with strawberries the size of apples.

They sat back in the deck chairs outside, bellies full, listening to the sounds of the birds chirping and tree frogs singing. It was the first time in months that she finally felt at peace and content. She closed her eyes and lost herself in the sounds all around her. Even the song of the crickets was calming and she quickly forgot, if only for a moment, that she wasn't at home.

They stayed outside for hours. When Woodrow finally spoke, he broke the spell and reality hit her again.

"Tell me about home."

"Home?" she asked.

"Tell me about it. What's it like?"

Cara thought for a moment. Memories flooded her, and she could feel herself getting homesick. She had never felt that way before, but somehow she was.

"It was... I don't know. It's home. What do you want to know?" she said, refusing to open herself up.

"Who was the one that stabbed you in the back?"

"You obviously have talked to Cynthia," Cara said, not meeting his eye-line.

"She called me before you got up this morning."

Cara nodded and pursed her lips.

"They are," she said, unsure what to say really. How could she admit what she really wanted to say, which was that they were horrible, but not sound awful herself?

"I used to feel like there was something special about me," Cara started. She remembered how before she moved to the new town, there was a dream of being a known photographer, but the new school and that group of girls had changed it all. Now, she wasn't so sure if she wanted to be known, not if it meant having to deal with people that could be so cruel to her.

"My mom always told me I was special, and for a long time, I believed it. I always thought I was going to be someone that people knew, you know? I remember dreaming that one day I would say my name and people would be shocked it was me. And I would just smile and sign my name on whatever they had ready, and that would be it."

Cara still remembered the day that her grandfather gave her his old Brown Target six-twenty camera. It was the one that he had taken all of his family photos with. She was over the moon and quickly jumped on the internet to figure out how to load the film. After taking a roll of pictures, she wasted no time in setting up a darkroom in her parent's shed. She loved watching the pictures appear in front of her out of the bottom of the photo trays.

Her words tumbled out of her and she told him all about it. Her photographs quickly replaced all the artwork in her parent's home.

She didn't even notice he was watching her until she finally opened her eyes and quickly wiped away a tear that had tried to escape her eyes.

"Sounds like something you really love. You should go after that."

"What does it matter? I won't be famous."

"But you could be if you tried. And even if you aren't, at least you'd be doing something you love," Woodrow said.

"I don't know," she said, feeling the heat rising in her chest.

Silence fell over them for a moment. Cara could tell that Woodrow didn't know what to say. He didn't know enough about her world to be able to say what would happen.

"Tell me more about this world," Cara said, looking back at him. "I found a book in my room and it told me how you got here, but that's it."

Woodrow sat back in his chair and sighed.

"Well, after that, we started building homes and made the city as it is now. And everything was great. We were free and at peace and it was all great times. Some parties that we used to have were amazing.

"Then one day, Sarith entered this world. She was pretty shy and quiet at the beginning, so we tried to make her feel welcome. We showed her everything and told her about how we do everything that we do, and she was so amazed. And at first, she totally joined in. We asked her if she wanted to go home many times, but she always said no. She wanted to stay and learn more. She made it sound like she didn't really have much to go home to. We didn't question it either.

"Things turned when she tried magic. It kept coming out wonky or without any real power. Everyone could see the frustration building in her. Honestly, from the moment she got here, all she wanted was to be one of us. She loved life here. But it took her months to get any form of magic. Once she figured it out, she did as much as she could, and loved it. Her magic was a very general kind and, well, she could do almost anything with it. She changed objects into other things; made plants grow; and made exquisite meals. She held weekly dinners where everyone in the town was invited, and everyone wanted to join and eat her food. It was the best we had ever tasted."

Woodrow shifted in his chair and looked over at Cara. She was watching him closely. James hadn't told her about this part. It seemed so strange to think of her as someone good.

"She wanted to join our teams in the dream-writing rooms. But a human writing human dreams? We weren't sure if that would be wise. So, with no real dream or passion, she eventually got restless. Eventually, doing all of this wasn't enough. She pushed herself harder and harder to do magical things that we had never even thought to try. She was trying to break boulders, make it rain on sunny days, and she even was trying to fly. With every failed attempt, she got angry. And it only grew. She would stomp a foot down on the ground and the whole earth around her would vibrate and soil would go everywhere. Any animals that were around her went flying.

"Slowly, we saw her personality change. She was becoming more and more harsh and didn't want to have the magic everyone else had: she wanted more.

"It was around that time that the beast appeared. I know James told you about how initially he was small. Each time she got upset, the thing grew. And not only that, her powers of magic also grew. She could do things we had never seen before. She was able to make people do things they didn't want to and manipulate things to her will.

"As she got stronger, we all got really scared. What if she turned against us? Eventually we approached and asked her about it and she got upset. She hurt one of our friends, badly. Then she disappeared. The beast went with her. And nothing was the same after that. She began capturing townspeople and turning them to her side. She built up an army and appointed a general ahead of them all to be sure they cooperate. For a long time, we didn't know what the plan was, but we wondered if it had something to do with the dreams.

"Next thing we know, the dreams start showing up in her handwriting and we are told to write them, and if we didn't, bad things would happen."

"Which is what is still happening now," Cara said, finishing his thought.

"Exactly."

"And as she continued to send the dreams, she only got stronger and took over more," Cara said.

"Yep. She took more townies and continued to get stronger. Now we believe that she's getting restless again as the dreams are getting worse, and the beast has grown over the last few months."

"So, you need someone to do something that you aren't capable of doing," Cara finished, letting her eyes finally reach his.

"No one is asking you to do anything."

"Hmm," she said, feeling herself beginning to shut down. It was very clear to her that they expected her to save them, but she was nothing like this woman. She wasn't strong.

Cara noticed that as they talked, the day had turned into night and all around her, crickets began to sing. Fireflies danced through the cool night air.

She didn't want to talk about this anymore. She really just needed to be alone with her thoughts. Every time she even thought she might be able to help them, she felt the ache in her side and stomach.

She looked at Woodrow as the thoughts dissipated and she excused herself. A lump grew in her throat and tears were threatening to escape. She made her way back into her room and slumped on the bed. Her head ached. All she wanted to do now was take a couple of painkillers and crawl into bed. She needed a moment of peace where she wasn't expected to do anything like saving the world.

She reached into the small closet and grabbed an extra blanket and threw it on the bed. As she adjusted it, she bumped the bedside table and something fell to the floor, thudding quietly against the hard clay. Peeking under the bed, she saw a small leather backpack. She picked it up and looked into it. It was empty except for a pocket comb.

She looked around. She had very little in this world, but there were the few pieces of clothing that she had been given. And there was the comb and she had a toothbrush in the other room. It was all so close. As the idea took hold, she grinned. She would take her next steps into her own hands.

Woodrow knocked at her door.

"I brought you a sandwich if you want one," he said.

"No thanks," she said, not wanting to see him. But then again, if she really was going to do this, she would need fuel. "Actually, I will take it," she said, stashing the bag in the closet before he opened the door.

"Oh, good." He opened the door and came in with a tray with the sandwich, a drink and an apple.

"I'm not that hungry right now, but I thought I might get hungry tonight."

"Oh yes, that makes sense."

He put it at the end of the bed and turned to leave. His steps were slow and heavy as he turned to the door.

"This has all been a bit much," she offered, not wanting him to be too defeated.

"I know."

"It's not that I want you animals to get hurt or bullied, but I just know I can't do anything to help you."

"You don't know until you try," he said, turning back to her. Even in the low light, his eyes twinkled with just an ounce of hope.

"I do know. Trust me. I do," she said.

Woodrow walked back into the living room and sat down at one of the chairs by the fireplace. It wasn't lit tonight, as it seemed extra warm.

Cara closed her door and let herself fall back against it. She took a deep breath and looked at the tray. There was a flower beside the plate the sandwich was on. It was gorgeous, so different from anything she had ever seen at home. It sparkled and shimmered with pinks and purples. She picked it up and smelled it. It was sweet like candy. Woodrow would have made that for her. She felt bad. Maybe she should stay. They all wanted to believe in her so badly. Could it really hurt to try?

Cara crawled into bed and pulled the covers up high. Maybe, in the fresh light of day, everything would seem better. Maybe she should try. She let her mind wander to this afternoon and the people she had met. They were so sweet to her. Her mind drifted back to home, but not where she lived now, but before they moved to the town that she had grown up in and loved more than anything. She hated she couldn't be there anymore. She knew they had to be where they were for now, but she wished she could go back.

She missed her friends. She wished she could see them again, and to feel like she actually belonged.

She could see them having fun at the movies, eating all the popcorn without her, and wishing she could be there.

Sleep crept its way into her thoughts and she felt herself drifting up and over them, watching them at a weird angle. She watched as they faded away and, without knowing it, she slipped into the darkness of sleep.

Eighteen

Sarith paced the room. Night had fallen, but sleep wasn't within her reach.

She walked out of her bedroom and waved off the guards that stood at her door, ignoring their questions. At first, she wandered aimlessly, but eventually she found herself in her own dream-writing room. She felt peaceful here, even despite the nightmares she wrote. Already she had sent the dreams over to those animals, and before the night was through, the typed dreams would show up in the magical boxes again, while the humans in the other world would be experiencing them. Grinning to herself, she opened the lid on one of the many boxes that sat around the room. It remained empty and she sighed.

She couldn't remember the last time that she had a dream. It would have been before she came here, but she had lost track of how long ago that was now. Sometimes she considered writing a dream for herself, just so she could feel something in her life again, but she never did. Now that she was the strongest being here, the challenge and tension she had in her old life was gone. She had almost everything she ever wanted while here. Sure, some of the animals didn't go along with what she said, but she would either eliminate them or force them to see her ways, and that was it.

And at first she loved it. Being in power was so intoxicating. But over time, the lack of any real challenge was annoying her. No one could come even close to her strength. No longer was there any fight, thrill, or challenge. Now she was getting bored.

She looked around the room and slid into the chair. The stack of thick ivory paper sat waiting for words to be written. She knew she was done for the night, but something about adding to it was so enticing right now. Maybe this would help her feel less restless.

But who would she write a dream for? She wished she could write one for one of those animals in town that bothered her so much, but no one here dreamed. It was the one thing that she couldn't get used to. She had asked the General and anyone she had captured initially, but all of them said the same thing; it wasn't possible for them to dream.

Leaned back in her chair, she sighed. She gathered her hair up and twisted it into a bun that she held in place while she thought.

That woman, she thought, repeatedly. She was the first person, other than herself, to come into this world and it struck her as so strange. Sarith wanted to see her, maybe even meet her. She wanted to know what this woman was all about. Was she here to take over? Or was she just going to leave? She hated not knowing. The General hadn't returned yet with any information, but she had to know. Did this woman have magic? And if so, was she going to use it against her?

Surely I'll be stronger, she mused, *but what if?*

Sarith laughed off the very hint of the idea. Of course she would win. She had been here for years, spending countless hours perfecting and honing her skills. This new person had been here a heartbeat in comparison. She let her hair fall around her shoulders again and shook it out.

She grabbed a piece of paper and held it up. What if she sent this woman a dream? They would have to write it. She would make sure of it, but could this woman actually receive a dream here?

The idea danced around for a moment. She would do it and see how this woman would react. Maybe that would bring her out of hiding with those creatures and lead to her knowing if she had magic.

She bent over the paper, pen poised for a moment, then began.

* * *

James looked across the heads of his fellow writers and watched as they meticulously typed out the dreams they had been sent. He saw the anguish on their faces, but knew there was very little he could do for them.

He headed over to the next table and picked up the stack of dreams already typed and carried them over to the enchanted boxes on the far wall. He lifted the lid and just as he was about to put the dreams in to send them back to Sarith, a paper appeared. Stunned, he put the stack down and carefully pulled the sheet out. Scanning the words, he glanced around to see if anyone had seen him. Realizing no one was watching, he put it down on the table, lifted the pile of completed dreams, and put them into the box. He closed the lid, but didn't take his eyes off the other page. Hastily, he folded the paper up and palmed it. With another glance around the room, he walked slowly, but with determination to his bedroom.

He quickly closed the door, leaving it open only slightly so he could hear if someone was coming near.

The paper he held couldn't be right. A dream to Cara? But no one in this world had dreamt before. She would literally be the first one ever to have one.

He fell into a chair at a table in the corner of his room. He tossed the sheet onto the table and paused. There was no way anyone else would type this for him.

He looked at the door again, and being sure that he heard no one coming, he carefully reached under the table and into a small hole in the wall that he had dug. Inside was a compact typewriter. He plopped it onto the table and fished into the hole again and found an envelope of enchanted paper and fed it through the typewriter.

He sat up and poised his hands over the keys, and took a deep breath. As he exhaled, he let his fingers start. The words he typed were so awful that he cringed and attempted to push them out of his mind. He shuttered and finished as fast as he could. Once done, he pulled the paper out and stashed the typewriter and the extra paper back in their hiding place.

James folded and palmed the page again and left the room. Scanning the room, it was clear no one missed him. Walking past another table, he grabbed the stack of dreams that had piled up and carried them over to the boxes. Unfolding the page, he put it on top and carefully placed it in the box and, with one last moment of hesitation, he closed the lid and walked away.

Nineteen

Relief washed over Cara as she looked around at all her new friends. They would finally be safe.

At her feet lay the body of Sarith. Her hair was sprayed out around her head like a dark starburst and blood slowly oozed out of one of her eyes. Sarith was gone and even though now she couldn't remember how she had done it, the evidence lay at her feet.

"Cara, how are we ever going to thank you?" Cynthia said, her eyes wide with excitement. A crowd gathered around her, gently pulling her away from the scene. Turning from the body, she walked until the lake came into view. The water shimmered and sparkled with the bright midday sun.

Cara looked into Cynthia's blue eyes, unsure what to say, then realized the sweet little rabbit that she was used to looking down to was suddenly her size. Cara shrugged it off and hugged her.

"Come! You must celebrate with us," Terrance said. He raised his paws up in the air and everyone around them cheered.

"I would love that," Cara said, letting her voice trail off.

"But you want to get home to your family," Terrance said, nodding. "I understand."

"Thank you for everything you've done for me." She gave him and Cynthia another hug and waved to the rest of her new friends. She would miss them so much. They had taught her more about herself than anyone else had. She would miss their friendship.

Cara blinked. She was home. In front of her was the deep red front door of her home. She suddenly felt so small. She grabbed the handle and pushed it open. It creaked loudly, echoing throughout the house.

The smell of decay hung in the air. She coughed and pulled her shirt up over her mouth and nose. Fear seeped into her bones. Something was wrong, terribly wrong, but any guesses she might have had seemed out of reach. Each step she took was harder than the last as she followed the smell up the staircase and down the hall towards her parents' bedroom. She didn't even have to open the door to know the truth. Time shifted and she was at the foot of the bed, her parents still in it, dead.

Cara turned away and retched, and once she started, she couldn't stop. She stumbled back down the hall, down the staircase and collapsed against that blood-red door. She pushed and shoved, but it held firm. Panic consumed her. She felt heat rising up her neck and into her ears. She had to get out of here. But the red door held firm. Cara suddenly realized she was screaming. It was a blood-curdling scream that didn't stop. She stood and banged her hands on the door over and over, trying to get it to open. She pounded on it until her fists bled red and continued smashing her blood into the cracks of the wood; the same colour as that damn blood-red door her mother had loved so much. She screamed again and again. Her legs gave out and she fell.

Tears so hot she thought they would burn her skin, poured down her cheeks. She may have won in that other world but the rippling effects had turned her own real world into a never-ending nightmare.

"This is not my home," she said, again and again to herself. "Not my home, not my home." She cried it over and over until she felt herself screaming it at the top of her lungs.

"Not my home!"

* * *

Cara awoke, drenched in cold sweat. She was screaming. Woodrow raced into her room and turned on a light. She was pale and even from the doorway, he saw the tremor in her hands.

"What's wrong? What happened?" Woodrow asked, fear making him shake now too.

Cara struggled to catch her breath. The images were still so vivid and haunted her. Woodrow ran to the kitchen and grabbed a glass of water. He handed it to her and watched as she held it carefully in both hands and slowly sipped at it.

He took it from her shaky hands and set it on the nearby table before sitting down on the edge of the bed.

"It was horrible," she said as her breathing calmed. She told him everything she had seen, pausing at times to catch her breath.

"You went home and saw this? How did you get there? And then back so quickly?" Woodrow asked, confusion clouding his face.

"Home? What are you talking about?" Cara asked.

"You went home and saw all this?" Woodrow said.

"No," Cara said, shaking her head. "No. I've been here. Why would you think I went home?"

"Well, where else could you have seen this?" Woodrow asked, clearly confused.

Cara looked at the wall behind him and let her eyes trace the crack that jutted out from the door trim. It reminded her of the tree branches from the painting in James's home.

"Woodrow, it was a dream: a horrible, horrible nightmare. Probably the worst I've ever had." Cara grabbed the glass again and took another sip. She wiped her soaked forehead with the edge of her nightshirt. The dream had felt so real. Usually first thing in the morning she could shake the images, but these ones wouldn't fade.

Woodrow stumbled off the bed and backed into the wall.

"You're mistaken," Woodrow said.

Cara looked at him and saw the colour drain from his face and his fluffy tail suddenly seemed disheveled.

"No, I know now it was just a dream. I'm okay," she said, waiting for the images to fade.

"That's not, that's not, no," he stammered. "You went home and saw this."

"No, it was a dream," Cara insisted. "What's wrong?" She watched as he crept around the edge of the room to the doorway, slowly backing away from her.

"You're scaring me! What's wrong!" she demanded.

"We don't have nightmares here," he managed to say, leaning up against the door.

"Well, you must. I just had one."

"No," he said, shaking his head.

"Woodrow, stop this. Of course, you have dreams and even nightmares."

"In all the years this town has existed, no one has ever had nightmares. By the time we finish writing all the dreams for humans, we don't have the time to write them for ourselves. No one has ever, ever had a dream here." He ran his paw over his head, frazzled. "I have to call James! I have to find out who did this to you!"

"Can it wait until morning?" Cara said, suddenly feeling very anxious about James knowing. Something didn't feel right at all. He was the one that supervised, yet somehow he missed this? She had heard him say there was more than just one Dream Writing room, so maybe it was someone else, but she couldn't get past the uneasy feeling that settled in her stomach.

"But he really should know," Woodrow said.

"Just until the morning. Let's get a good sleep. Maybe in the light of day we'll be able to think more clearly about it?" Cara knew she was grasping at straws, but she just wanted a bit more time to think.

"Sure," he hesitantly agreed, but she could tell that he didn't love the idea.

"Do you want me to stay with you for a bit? At least until the images fade?" Woodrow was asking.

The images had faded, but she knew it would take some time for them to be completely gone.

"I'll be okay. You don't have to stay," she found herself saying, but she knew that wasn't what she truly wanted.

"Okay. I'll be in the other room if you need me." He walked out of the room and paused to look back at her. He nodded just once before heading to his bedroom.

Cara watched him go before she got up and closed her door.

Twenty

Cara looked at the window, the curtains gently swaying with the breeze. Sleep was not coming for her. Those images from her dream still haunted her. Every time her eyelids closed, she would see her parents lifeless bodies in the bed. Then she would bolt up and look around, reassuring herself that it was just a picture, and not reality.

She got up and paced the room, treading lightly to not wake Woodrow. Everything felt so wrong. Sure, she had met some great folks here, but this was unreal. Memories threatened to drown her. She thought back to the Hammer and wondered how far she would have gone. Maybe she had been grabbed and pulled out of the water after all, and now she was in a coma. Or maybe it was something worse. Was she dead? She didn't feel dead. She could remember swimming through the tunnel and her lungs burning from needing oxygen. It had all felt so real.

She winced as she pressed on her still bruised stomach. The injury was unquestionably real. And if this was actually all real, then she was in severe danger. They all were.

That woman and her beast would not only pursue her, but once they found her, would they kill her? She didn't know, but she didn't want to find out. To her right was a closet with the door ajar. Peeking out of it was a backpack strap. She threw the door open and grabbed the bag. A handkerchief was on the bedside table. She wrapped up the sandwich and tossed the apple in the bag with it. She sat on the bed until the clock chimed midnight. Woodrow had already shut off everything for the night. The only visible light emanated from the fireplace's glowing embers.

She tiptoed out into the kitchen and grabbed another apple and a small container that she filled with water. In one drawer she found a pack of matches, which she stuffed into the bag. Taking once last glance around, she grabbed her shoes, she slipped outside, and quietly closed the door.

Cara tossed her shoes to the ground before rubbing the bumps on her arms away. She sat on the cool stones and fumbled to put her feet in the grey sneakers. Her shaky hands tied the laces into a lopsided bow that reminded her of Cynthia's ears, but she shook off the thought.

"This is it," she mumbled to herself as she peaked around the corner of the house to the main road. The pub down the street was lit up, but everything else was quiet.

She walked down the cobblestone street and past the fountain towards the edge of town. At this late hour, only the moon and crickets were out. In the distance, the guards stood laughing and joking around with each other, ignoring the gate. She cautiously slipped through it and, once out of sight, she quickened her pace until she was running as fast as her feet would let her, adrenaline leading her on. She tried to recall the passage to the lake, but everything felt so different under the velvet light of the moon.

Her feet slipped and stumbled over loose rocks and bits of moss. Fog was rolling in, muting the moonlight. She spun around. The mountain was gone. Everything looked the same now. She slowed down, spinning in circles. Which way had she come? She had no idea anymore. A wave of anxiety washed over her as thoughts of the beast crept back in. She tumbled again, falling hard, her ankle twisting in pain. She choked on a cry.

Cara sat down on the mossy ground, the bark of the tree scratching at her back. Her ears rang over the silence as her head cleared. Testing out her ankle, she turned it without too much pain.

Suddenly, the sky lit up so brightly, Cara saw spots. The tree branches stretched out like arthritic fingers overhead. A loud crash of thunder made her jump.

The forest was unforgiving. She ran, slowing as she stumbled over logs and roots, her breath ragged.

The air chilled suddenly. Another flash of lightning. Thunder clapped.

When the rain started, it fell like a sheet, instantly soaking her to the bone. Her hair clung to her face in wavy rivers. Finding the lake like this would be nearly impossible. If only she'd asked Woodrow for help, maybe she wouldn't be in this mess.

Lightning again. Ahead, she saw an enormous figure. Cara's heart raced. Was it the beast? Another flash outlined the jagged tops of the mountain. When had she come this close to it? The trees on that side towered so high she couldn't see far. She approached the mountainside and saw an edge jutting out. It was the front of a small cave where she would get some relief from the rain. She wiped her face with her wet hand, trying to clear her vision.

Cara darted inside. The smell of decaying leaves and fresh rain filled her lungs. A pile of leaves had blown into one corner. It wouldn't be the best of a bed, but it would be something. She pulled out all the clothes packed in the bag and laid them out across the rock floor in the hopes they would somewhat dry so she could change. The cave was cold, and she couldn't stop herself from shaking.

She poured out the rest of her bag. She knew it was in here somewhere. Under the sandwich and fruit, she found what she was looking for: the match book she had packed. She carefully picked it up and looked it over. Even in the low light, she could tell the box was still dry. She slowly slid it open. To her dismay, it only had one match. She cursed under her breath. Why hadn't she checked that? She carefully picked it up. It was too dark to see very far, so she put her hands on the floor and shuffled back and forth, looking for any kind of stick she could make a fire with.

Another flash of lightning.

Making a crude tee-pee, she grabbed some bark off a nearby stick and stuffed it inside. Risking a smokey fire, she added a handful of leaves. She grabbed the bag again and searched each pocket carefully. Buried deep in the inside pocket, she found a pamphlet for the gallery. She crumpled it up and stuffed it deep inside the tee-pee. That was really her only chance of a fire truly catching.

Cara took a deep breath and struck the match on a rock and saw it slowly come to life. She steadied her hands and carefully took it to the piece of paper and waited. The flames grew and consumed the paper. This will work, she thought as she dropped the match in and held her hands out to it. The warmth felt good. She let herself sit and soak it all in. Her clothes would dry and she might get some sleep. Then in the morning, in the fresh light of day, she would find her way to the lake and go home.

She turned and grabbed the bottle of water and took a swig. She would need to save some for tomorrow, unless she could funnel some of the persistent rain. Setting the bottle outside with the lid open, she hoped some would make its way in there. She knew she should try to sleep. She would need to rest before going out again the next day.

Suddenly, her back chilled and she spun. The fire had gone out. A small trail of smoke rose up.

"No, no, no, no!" she cried out. She gently blew into the tee-pee, trying to revive it, but she watched as the dried edges of the leaves just floated away.

"No! Damn it! No!" She stood up and looked down at the smouldering trigs. She stomped her foot down, the vibration of it making the tee-pee fall apart. Rage filled her and she kicked it hard, sending the sticks flying everywhere. Stomping over to the pile of leaves, she climbed in. Hopefully, they would dry her out and keep her warm.

Cara buried herself deep inside the bed of leaves, letting them cover her almost completely before she finally let herself relax as best she could. The storm raged outside, howling in anger. She hoped sleep would come, but she knew it would be slow in taking her away.

* * *

Cara turned over again and again. Images of things that likely would come to be with this beast played on her mind. She could see this thing causing nothing but destruction to these animals that she was now starting to actually care about. Were they actually her friends at this point? She wasn't sure, but she knew she cared for them, even if it was just in a small way.

James had saved her life that first day, and Woodrow had made her feel welcome and at home since. They had accepted her into this world without thinking twice. It didn't matter that she was human. A ping of guilt came over her but she quickly pushed it aside.

Shivering again, she kicked herself for not checking for more matches. She thought she was going to get to the lake tonight and wouldn't even need them. She only brought them, just in case. And now, she lay there in the dark, covered in leaves, trying to get warm.

If she were at home, she would be in her soft, cozy bed just smothered in thick blankets, her body warm and her feet dry. She would wake up in the morning, eat a big breakfast of bacon, eggs and ham and drink the hottest cup of tea she could handle.

But then her mind drifted to school. The Hammer appeared in her mind. Those eyes filled her with dread. They were the darkest eyes she had ever seen: so cold and uncaring.

The pile of sticks that once was the teepee still lay where she had kicked it over. She wished she hadn't let it die, and that she could feel the warmth of a nice big fire. In fact, anywhere warm would be better. Looking at it, she willed it light. Everyone else in this place has magic, so why not her? Focusing as best as she could against her chattering teeth, she pictured the flames coming up and rising, warming her body. She could almost feel it. The heat of it, soothing her body and making her feel better.

But no amount of wishing or wanting made a spark appear. She closed her eyes, resigned, and sighed. How silly was it for her to think that she would have magic after just getting here?

Sleep will have to come soon, she thought. When it finally came over her, it was a light sleep, plagued with thoughts of what could come.

And in front of her, as the rain and winds continued, one stick in the pile glimmered and grew deep red, if only briefly before going out once more.

Twenty-One

Woodrow sipped his coffee and glanced for the tenth time at Cara's door. It was nearing eleven o'clock in the morning. Knowing she had a rough couple of days, he still thought she would be ready for breakfast by now.

Should I knock on the door or wait it out? he wondered. His brain was having trouble thinking after consuming three cups of coffee. He wasn't accustomed to having a human in his place.

He rose, sat, smoothed his fur, and sipped. Standing up once more, he emptied the remaining contents of his mug down the drain.

Inhaling deeply, he walked towards the phone. Maybe he should call James. He might have an idea what to do. Slowly, he grabbed the phone and dialed, waiting between each number, hoping she might come out.

The phone rang only once before James answered.

"Yes?" James answered.

"It's Woodrow."

"Oh," he said, distraction clouding his voice, "what's going on?"

"Were you expecting someone else?"

"Uh, no, it's fine," he said. His voice came back clearer and more focused. "What's going on? What are you and our guest doing today?"

"That's actually why I'm calling. She's still sleeping. She hasn't come out yet. And I'm getting a bit concerned."

"What are you talking about? Have you knocked on her door?"

"I didn't want to disturb her."

"Well, go in there and find out what's going on! Or at the very least, knock. Keep me on the phone."

"Okay."

Woodrow tucked the phone between his shoulder and chin, and walked over to her room, watching the cable slowly stretch out. He knocked loudly and waited.

Nothing.

He knocked again.

"Cara? You okay in there?"

"Open the door," James said in the earpiece.

"What if she's not dressed?"

"Woodrow, open the damn door!"

Stunned, Woodrow opened the door slowly, it creaking loudly against the stillness of his house.

"She's gone, isn't she?" James said.

The door revealed the perfectly made bed and the closet left open. Woodrow let the phone fall as he walked in and scanned the room.

"She's gone," he finally said to James after gathering the phone back.

"Damn it!"

"James, we have to find her! What if the beast gets her?"

"What if she tries to go home!" James exclaimed.

"James, there's something else I need to tell you," Woodrow said.

"What's that?" James asked, sounding agitated.

"She had a nightmare last night."

"What?" he shouted.

Woodrow jumped back, but then composed himself.

"She had a nightmare and woke up completely frantic. I calmed her down and I really thought she was going to be fine otherwise I would have said something. I don't know who sent it. You'll need to find out who did," Woodrow said.

"I'll find out what I can. We need to look for her and find her before it gets dark tonight," he said.

"And how do you suppose we do that? It's been raining since last night and hasn't stopped. Her scent will be long gone. There's no way anyone can track her."

After a long pause, James finally spoke.

"I'm coming over. Wait until I get there. We will go out together and find her. Don't tell anyone."

Woodrow agreed and hung up the phone.

Twenty-Two

"She has to be at the lake," Woodrow said to James once he burst through the door.

James didn't stop. He stormed into the bedroom, checking the closet and the bed.

He pushed past Woodrow and looked at the front door. He quickly noticed her shoes were missing.

"She didn't sneak out the window. She took her shoes."

"What do we do now?" Woodrow asked, wringing his paws.

"We search for her," James said, his fur sticking out at weird angles. It clearly wasn't brushed. He never left the house unless it was perfect. "She wasn't at my place this morning, given I can't imagine she would be able to find her way there even if she tried. Like you said, she's probably gone to the lake. I want you to stay in town and ask the others that went to the art gallery yesterday and see if she showed up there. Maybe she went to one of them for help. I'm going to head to the lake and see if I can find some kind of trail. There is always that chance that I might find something. We have to find her."

Woodrow turned to his friend and nodded.

"We need to meet up later after we search," Woodrow said, getting his coat and umbrella.

"We'll meet at eight. That will give us the day to ask around, and will give me a chance to check the lake and a few other places between there and here," James said. "You go ahead. I'll lock up for you."

Woodrow agreed, darting outside and disappeared.

* * *

James watched as Woodrow hurried out the front door and headed towards the centre of town.

He grabbed the phone.

"She's missing," he whispered into the phone. "I think she's headed to the lake. I'll find her," he said quickly before hanging up and heading to the door.

Twenty-Three

Cara woke, the sound of the rain still echoing through the cave. She stood and stretched, her head spinning. She needed to eat. Grabbing the sandwich she brought, she devoured it. Once she found the lake, she would eat an apple before jumping into the water and getting herself home.

The clothes she had laid out the night before were now dry. She changed, the fabric stiff and scratchy against her skin. She stuffed the rest of her things into the bag again.

Cara had hoped that in the morning light, she would have been able to see more, but a thick mist hung in the air. The rain hadn't stopped, so she knew the terrain would be exhausting, but she had to do it. She had to get herself home.

Cara stepped out from the cave and into the forest. She snuck through the trees and walked away from the cave, every so often breaking tree branches along the way. That way, if she got hopelessly lost, at least she could follow her path back to the cave and start over.

The mist covered her skin and instantly made her feel damp again.

Shifting the bag across her body, she wiped the moisture off her face and looked up. There was no way of seeing the mountain through all this forest, but she knew it was still on her right.

Eventually, she would have to head to her left, leaving the safety of the mountain, but the unknown frightened her. The lake was somewhere over there, but she couldn't remember exactly where. She pushed herself to walk away from the mountain and towards what she hoped was the lake. Maybe if she just kept moving, she would eventually find it, but she was terrified. Leaving didn't sound so good now, after all.

* * *

Cara had been walking for hours. The trees all looked the same. A cool breeze blew over her, and night was closing in. Her stomach wouldn't relent. The sandwich and apple she had packed earlier were long gone, and she had found nothing else since.

She needed to find somewhere to rest before daylight was fully gone. Her feet ached in spots that she didn't even know could hurt. Leaning against a tree, she took shelter under the thick branches. Her legs tingled against the chill that had seeped into them.

She slid down the tree and fell to the ground. If she wasn't so numb, it would have hurt to hit the ground that hard, but she was so cold, she barely felt it.

The fog was letting up, but she could hear a bigger storm coming. The sky was electric and the next wave of the storm would be fierce. As the world around her quietened, a voice came to her and sent more shivers down her spine than the cold ground was already doing. It was unlike any other that she had heard in this place so far.

"I don't know what is taking so long to find her, but she has to be either coming here or staying with someone."

"I don't know," someone else said.

Cara knew without even seeing the face that the one figure was Sarith. She shifted slightly and peered around the tree. Not even twenty feet away, she saw the long, dark, soaked hair stuck to the woman's back. Cara couldn't make out who was with Sarith, but she suspected it was General Barabus.

"Good. I will be at the castle and don't come back until you find her! Once you know where she is, we'll attack," Sarith said, hitting something on the ground. Vibrations from it radiated out around her and Cara felt a wave of heat wash over her.

Sarith walked past the animal and veered to the left, while the animal headed the other way and disappeared amongst the trees.

The gravity of the danger she was in hit her, but maybe if she followed the animal, she could find the lake. She stood on shaky legs and started to walk.

Twenty-Four

Woodrow spent the afternoon knocking on doors, asking if they had seen Cara. Each 'no' came like a hit to the gut. What if the beast had found her? What if Sarith already had her and was doing horrible things? He didn't know what to do if she was gone. She was really the only hope they had. If it wasn't her, then who else would defeat Sarith for them and end this reign of terror?

He walked through town, barely able to focus. James had said he was going to the lake and Woodrow wondered if he should have gone there too. It would make the most sense that she would be there, of course. She didn't want to be the hero. And she didn't think she would be. He wished she could believe in herself even if only a little bit because so many others did. In fact, most of who he had stopped to talk to that day believed she was the one. They all could feel it. So, what if that was true? If she could only let herself try before giving up, then maybe she would see what they all could already see.

Woodrow headed towards home. He could see the evening twilight coming, and he knew he would have to stop searching shortly. Hopefully, James would have good news.

Twenty-Five

Cara kept her distance as she followed the other animal. Her whole body ached, and she wanted more than anything to stop, but this might be her only real chance to find the way home.

The wind shifted suddenly and then stopped. Everything became so quiet. She stopped walking. Thunder clapped loudly, vibrating her very core. Lightning flashed, making spots appear before her eyes.

In that moment, when the earth was lit, she finally saw where she was. The lake was in front of her and she could see the bridge at the far side. She sighed heavily, her knees giving out and she fell to the soft earth below her. Finally, she had made it. The dark light was difficult to see through and she couldn't find the animal anymore. She hung back and waited for the lighting to give her sight once more.

Thunder clapped again.

If she was right, home could be right there, under that inky water. But she knew that if she truly wanted to go home, she would have to wait until this storm passed. Her eyes scanned the area again and out of the corner of her eye, she saw a cloaked figure walking towards the lake. She ducked back deeper into the shadows, but kept close.

The animal moved with a determined steadiness. She watched as he slowly dipped his head into the water, and a moment later, a large fish surfaced.

"Who else have you told about this, Seth?" she heard the figure ask as she crouched down. He was looking down towards the wet sand underfoot. He let his feet drag around in it, leaving wet trails that the lake slowly filled back up with little pools of water.

"No one. It's just me and the others here."

"That's very good," he said, glancing back at Seth. She watched as the fish dipped down into the water to catch his breath and reappeared as a flash of lightning lit up the sky, illuminating everything in its fierce light before plugging it into darkness. Even in that moment, Cara saw the gills on the fish gleam and flicker like coins at the bottom of a wishing well.

Thunder cracked and sent vibrations across the water. Rings rolled to the edge of the water and back again towards the fish. The sky finally let loose and rain pelted them in fat drops that soaked them.

"You should really think about taking cover," Seth said. "This storm is right above us. It's not safe. I need to get down so I don't get hit either."

"Just one more moment of your time. Have you met my friend? Liam!" he called out, and from behind a large tree nearby, a black bear emerged. Cara gasped. She had been there only moments before. One arm hung at his side, while the other stayed behind his back. He swaggered over and stood beside the figure.

"Nice to meet you," he said, an uneasiness taking over his voice, "but I really think you two need to take cover."

"Oh, we will. We just have one more thing to show you."

Liam slowly pulled his arm out from behind him and in another flash of lighting, Seth and Cara saw a shiny metal rod. It was almost as long as he was tall.

"W-what's that for?" Seth said, his expression completely changing. Another flash of lightning and pure fear filled his face.

"Well, you see, Cara mustn't know," the figure replied.

"I won't tell anyone. I can keep quiet," Seth pleaded.

"Now, I believe you, to some degree, but your friends down there? Not so much. They are too much of a liability. There is always one with a mouth on them that is just a bit too big and a bit too loose. And I have my orders to terminate you."

"Please no! I promise we won't talk. There must be another way," Seth said.

"I'm just following orders."

"But if they see us all dead and gone, won't they suspect something?" Seth asked, pleading in his eyes.

"It was an act of mother nature!" The figure continued. "Why would they ever suspect anything else?" He let out a laugh.

Another crack of thunder rang out, echoing across the open space.

Liam took a few big strides into the water and plunged the rod deep into the sticky mud below. Cara stood and felt her stomach turn. He was going to kill them all to protect information from getting to her. She took a step forward and saw the figure laugh, throwing his head back. She stopped. Her legs felt frozen. He would kill her if she tried to stop it, but how could she not?

Seth leapt out of the water. A screech escaped his lips unlike anything she had ever heard before. He hit the water again, his eyes blazing. The fish disappeared beneath the surface, then the figure walked back to the grass-line and stopped.

The sky light up again and again. The storm was over them. Thunder crackled and shook them. She would have to act fast. She took another two steps and then, flash!

The pole lit up and electricity spider-webbed out like gnarled fingers to the far ends of the lake. Cara fell back to the grass, and even at this distance, she could feel the heat coming from the strike. A moment later, all across the water, the fish of the lake slowly surfaced, bellies up, eyes hollow and vacant.

"Go," the figure said, gesturing to Liam to get the pole.

He grabbed it and brought it back over.

"Get rid of it. Don't let anyone see you with it. And if anyone asks, this was an unfortunate accident."

"Yes, sir," Liam replied.

The figure watched as Liam disappeared into the woods. He turned back and scanned the surface of the water and saw Seth's remains at the far end of the water. He paused only for a moment before he turned and left.

* * *

With wobbly legs, Cara emerged from the woods and made her way around the bridge. She stopped at the edge of the water. The storm was slowing down as it moved off into the distance.

The sight before her turned her stomach. She retched, then fell back into the soft, wet mud and cried hot, piercing tears. It may be a place that writes human dreams, but they also had their own version of nightmares here.

This had to be the work of Sarith. She knew that woman was terrorizing them, but she didn't know it was this bad. No one had told her it was this bad.

She needed to get back to Woodrow's. Maybe there she would at least be safe from whoever that was.

She tested her legs again and found they held, so she backed away slowly towards the woods. When she reached them, Cara turned and ran as quickly as she could manage. Her feet kept slipping on the slick mud, but she pushed on.

It was easier than she expected to find her way back to the cave using the trail she had made. The remains of the fire tee-pee were still there and she kicked it again in anger. She stopped only long enough to catch her breath, before following the mountain back around and hopefully back towards the town.

Eventually, she found the edge of town. The roads now seemed so familiar and comforting. Everything was quiet at this time of night, but she saw lights throughout. Her

legs ached as she finally reached the door that she currently called home and even though it had only been about
twenty-four hours since she had left, it felt so much longer.
Opening the door as quietly as it would allow, she slipped
inside. She didn't see Woodrow, but his door was open
and she could hear him snoring in the other room. She
wondered if he was sleeping well or not. Then she heard
him cry out and she froze. She wasn't ready to see him yet.
She needed to process all she had seen and to sleep. Oh,
how she longed for sleep. Her breathing was ragged and
her heart raced, not only from the running, but from fear.
How was she going to tell them all what she had seen?
Cara hoped they would be kind to her, but she didn't
know what to expect. For now, she slipped off her shoes
and snuck into her room, closing the door as quietly as she
could.

Even though she knew she wouldn't sleep for a while,
when she finally did, she hoped beyond all hope that she
wouldn't dream. Maybe tonight, being in this place, they
wouldn't make her dream.

Twenty-Six

"So, did that human see what we did?" Sarith asked, pausing her work on that day's nightmares.

The General smiled at her delighted.

"Oh, she did. Liam said he saw her running back to town. She looked terrified." Barabus walked over to the edge of the table to the stack she had just finished. He picked it up and took it over to the enchanted boxes. Lifting one lid, he placed them inside, closing it gently. The box glowed gold for a moment before returning to its original brown. He opened it again and the box was empty.

"Good." Sarith rubbed her hands together and laughed. She knew she would find this fun, but this game of cat and mouse was almost better than she had expected.

"What's the next step?" General Barabus asked, almost giddy with anticipation. He loved this game as much as Sarith.

"I want to see what she does now. She's had the night-mare, and she saw her way home endangered. I need her to get her magic going. Does she have any yet?"

"Not that I've seen. I watched her wander around the same thirty-foot circle for almost a full day. If she had magic, she would have been to the lake much earlier."

"This woman is stubborn," Sarith said, pondering. "Maybe we need to do something to her dear, sweet friends she has there. If I'm going to battle and crush her, she has to have magic. I want a worthy opponent, not like the animals here, no offence," she said, chuckling.

"I understand," he said, walking back over and looking over her shoulder at the page she had been writing when he came in. It was full of blood, gore, and death; every-thing that Sarith loved to fill the nightmares with.

"I have the perfect idea. Who's she been spending time with there?" Sarith asked.

"Woodrow, the twins Michael and Anthony, Cynthia, James, and just a scattering of others. But mostly the coun-cil members."

"I know what needs to be done," Sarith said, rising from her chair and walking out of the room. She would scare that woman into using magic, even if it meant destroying all her little friends. And she knew just who to do it to. Those precious twins that everyone loved so much, they would feel her wrath. Then, she would have her battle with Cara, and she would enjoy the moment she felt Cara's life being drained out of her body.

Twenty-Seven

Cara's eyes burned as she slowly opened them. She had only slept for a couple hours before she heard Woodrow talking on the phone. She could tell he was trying to be quiet to let her sleep, but her nerves were shot. Every sound through the night had made her jump.

She pulled her body from the bed and clumsily got herself dressed. She wanted to let herself fall back into the soft, comforting blankets, but Woodrow deserved to know the truth and if she was okay.

She steadily walked to the kitchen and found he had already begun a pot of tea. Without asking how long it was steeping, she grabbed a cup and poured herself some. The powerful aroma hit her. She hoped it would be enough to pull her out of this groggy state.

It was hot, almost too hot to drink, but she didn't care. She could feel Woodrow eyeing her, but she refused to meet his eyes. She needed a minute to figure out how she would tell him everything.

She could only imagine how she looked with her eyes blood-shot and her hair a complete mess. It must have been rough, because he said nothing and let her get her bearings first.

He placed a plate of food down in front of her and sat. He quietly began eating.

When she finally took a bite, he sat back and watched.

"I know you're probably mad," she said between bites of waffles drenched in maple syrup.

"I woke up around four this morning and saw your door closed when I had left it open last night. Then I saw your shoes and I knew you must be back."

"Yeah."

"Cara, where were you? You know how dangerous it can be around here with the beast, especially for—," he said, his words trailing off. The air was thick with the one word left unspoken.

"A human, you mean," Cara finally said, sitting back in her chair.

"Well, yes, but for anyone really, that is on their own. With Sarith looking for you, it's really not safe to chance being out in the open."

Cara took another drink and set it down. She didn't even want to meet his eyes, but she knew he would be glaring at her.

"So, are you going to tell me where you went?"

"I... I went to the lake. I was trying to get home."

"Okay. You obviously didn't go though," Woodrow said.

"I, um, I didn't go," she coughed, "I didn't go because —" She didn't know how she would tell him. The night she had been through was almost too much to bear.

"What happened?" he asked, as concern washed over him.

Cara felt her stomach turn. The image of the dead fish floating, their eyes vacant and hollow, haunted her. She pushed the plate away and sat up straighter.

The door burst open and in ran James. He was flustered and worry lines wrinkled his brow.

"James? What's wrong?" Woodrow asked, darting to his feet.

"There's been a tragedy."

* * *

James's eyes darted around the room. His fur was ruffled and his clothes were a mess. He walked over to the fireplace and warmed his paws for a moment before turning back to them. He stomped over to the chair across the room and sat down.

As James recounted the scene at the lake, Cara walked away, leaving them in the living room and went back to the kitchen to pour herself another cup of tea. Even without looking, she could feel their eyes on her. When she heard the conversation go quiet, she turned and returned their gaze.

"That's where you were last night, wasn't it?" James asked.

"Yes."

"Did you see it happen?" he asked, pulling at his shirt and smoothing it out.

Cara watched him. He seemed to have calmed his nerves pretty fast.

"I did. I was at the edge of the woods, although I didn't get a good look at who did it. I only heard one name. Liam. Do you know who that is?"

Woodrow stood at the name and rang his hands.

"What is it?" she asked.

"He's one of our friends that went missing. He's obviously working for her now," Woodrow said, visibly upset by the news. "Well, now what do we do?"

"The lake is roped off for right now. The vultures are on their way so they can clean up the mess. Once that's done, we'll be able to relocate others into the water we hope, but it's going to be a while before that can happen. We want to let the water rest for a couple of days at least."

"So, does that mean my way of getting home is gone?" Cara felt so selfish in asking when they had just lost their friends, but she had to know.

"At this point, we don't know. Sarith is obviously wanting you to stay," James said.

Cara felt a lump of tears growing in her throat.

"I'm sorry Cara. He's right though. I think it might be best if you stay put for a bit," Woodrow said.

Cara struggled to find her voice. She wanted to say something, but the lump made it impossible. For now she would stay but she wouldn't give up the idea of going home yet.

"There's something else," she said, looking down at the floor.

"What?" Woodrow asked, coming over to her.

"I saw Sarith," she whispered.

"How?" James demanded.

"I got so horribly lost on my way to the lake. Before I even reached it, I saw her and, I think, General Barabus, talking. They said that once they find me, they are going to attack."

"We have to move you then!" Woodrow said. He looked around his place frantically.

"Where would we move her to?" James shouted.

Woodrow jumped back, his tail low after being scolded.

"Woodrow, where would we move her to?" he said, more calmly again as he smoothed his fur. "She's in more danger at my place, so that's out. We're not moving her out of town. The next place around here is miles away and we would be seen or found long before we got there. The only thing we can do is have her stay here and keep her out of sight."

"Should the rest of the town stay out of sight? Should we do a lockdown?" Woodrow asked.

"Not a full lockdown," James said. "If we do that and Sarith, or any of her other people, come looking, they will know she's here. We need to keep the town mostly as normal, but keep her out of sight. Even if that just means her being disguised for now." He headed for the door and opened it wide.

"What are you doing? We need to talk about this more. We need to figure out a disguise, at least for her. Especially if she's going to try to, you know…"

"Listen, I have to get back. I can't stay here. There are things to do and I have to make sure the dreams are still going forward like nothing has happened, but I'll be back a bit later," James said.

"That's why you have the assistant supervisor! He can take care of it all!" Woodrow said. He couldn't understand his friend. Could he not leave things for even just a bit? Was he that obsessed?

"I can't. I have to do this myself. Keep her close. And find out if she has magic."

Woodrow glanced at him, but something was different.

James left without another word.

"That was, uh," Cara stuttered.

"Strange? Yeah, it was. It makes sense though, right? He can't chance anything looking different until we know more."

"About me and magic," Cara said, matter-of-factly.

"Yes. Exactly."

Cara shook her head. It was going to be harder than she thought to get these animals to accept the truth. Maybe making a fool out of herself trying would finally make them understand. She hated the idea, but maybe then she would finally be given the chance to go home.

Twenty-Eight

"So, I sent out a call to a few friends, and they dropped off some items for you," Woodrow said a few hours later as Cara came out of the bathroom.

His dining room table was now covered in everything from hats, coats, and sweaters, to shoes and gloves.

"What's all this for?" Cara asked.

"Well, like James said, we need to keep you out of sight, but I also want you to come with me. I have a few people I want you to meet."

Cara shifted through the pile and picked out a hat, a jacket, and some sunglasses.

Woodrow chuckled when she came out of her room, dressed up, but offered her his arm and she hooked arms with him, laughing along with him and walking out the door.

Woodrow and Cara walked to the market set up in the square around the fountain. There were tables full of fruits, vegetables, and handmade goods. Animals stood by their booths, talking to potential customers. The air was energetic.

As they wandered around the booths, they filled bag upon bag with produce and various nuts, seeds, and dried fruit the vendors were selling. It wasn't until Woodrow's bags were near bursting that he finally told her he was good and they left. Woodrow put the bags down and put his paws above them and closed his eyes a moment before the bags lifted and Woodrow and Cara followed them.

"Where are we going?" she asked.

"You'll see," he said, leading them back towards the entrance of town. Cara felt her anxiety rising, being this close to the edge of town, especially knowing Sarith was getting closer to finding her.

They turned down the last street and walked right into the twins from the cafe earlier. Cara instantly wanted to disappear. She couldn't face them yet. She had just left them in the worst possible way. Cara turned and tried to hide near a doorway, but it was too late; they had seen her.

"Hey!" Anthony said, smiling.

"Hey," Woodrow replied, looking over to Cara. She shot him a look, but he had already looked back at the twins. Her hands went clammy and she quickly rubbed them on her pants. She saw their eyes follow her hands, but they just looked back at Woodrow.

"What are you two up to now?"

Woodrow motioned to the bags of produce they had and the pair of them nodded.

Michael tried to make eye contact with Cara, but she kept her eyes down. She could still feel them, but she just wanted to slip away and not talk about it.

"Ah yes, I guess we forgot what day it was," Anthony said.

"Yes, if you'll excuse us." Woodrow went to take another step, but Anthony spoke up.

"Wait."

Cara finally looked up at them, wondering why he would stop them. She locked eyes with Michael, who winked at her and mouthed the words, "It's okay." He made a funny face as Anthony leaned in to talk to Woodrow. She chuckled. They both turned to her and Michael, but continued talking. Maybe they weren't as mad as she thought they would be.

"So, I set up this really great campfire spot, about ten minutes into the woods, just by the old McGregor place. I was thinking about testing it out tonight after a few snacks at the pub. Any chance you guys might want to join us?"

Cara loved campfires. They always reminded her of the times she went camping with her aunt at her cottage. She loved the smell of the burning wood and the heat that radiated from it, warming her face until it felt like it might burn. There was something so comforting about it. It was like a fiery embrace that made her feel at home.

"I would love that," Cara said, before Woodrow could answer. He was surprised but agreed.

"How about we meet up at the pub around eight, then?" Woodrow said.

The twins jumped in delight and turned the corner back towards town.

The street they were on only had a few small homes and a couple of them barely looked big enough for Woodrow and Cara to get in. They stopped in front of one that looked only big enough for a mouse.

She looked at him, puzzled, but he just kept focused.

"Hold on a moment." Woodrow reached into the bag and grabbed a block of cheese. He broke it in half and put the bag gently on the ground. He looked over at Cara and grabbed her hand. She tried to pull it away, but he held firm and said something she couldn't quite make out before they suddenly were face to face with the small doorway. He let go of Cara's hand and knocked on the wooden door.

Cara looked around, stunned. They were now the size of mice. The street suddenly seemed to tower over them. All the houses that were once almost too small now were bigger than mansions.

The small door of the home opened.

A grey dormouse opened the door and laughed.

"Woodrow you sneak! You're early! Come in, come in." The mouse looked at Cara surprised, but held the door open for the two of them as they entered.

"What do you have today, my friend?" the mouse said.

"Some homemade old fort cheddar. You're favourite." Woodrow handed it over and walked across the room. In the one corner sat a bed. It was covered in ruffled blankets. She watched as he walked over and sat on the edge of it and said a quiet hello.

A tiny mouse sat up and threw its arms around Woodrow. He hugged him back and immediately the mouse started a story about a knight, a princess, and a dragon that held the princess captive. Cara had heard that same story about a million times before in her storybooks as a kid, but hearing this little one telling it made it seemed brand new. She got caught up in the tale and, without realizing it, she came over and sat on the bed too.

"And then the dragon, he uh, he roared so loud the knight's helmet went flying off his head and he thought he was going to die! But he, he, he just went up to that dragon and he waved his finger at him and told him to stop! He was being a bad dragon. And that he was going to save the princess, and he needed to let him."

"What happened then?" Woodrow asked, moving closer to the storyteller and his eyes growing wide.

"That dragon, he, he said okay!" The little mouse laughed and so did Woodrow, both of them grabbing their stomachs with fits of laughter.

Cara was confused. She didn't see how that was funny as it definitely wasn't the ending she was used to, but seeing them laughing, she couldn't stop herself. She started and so did the mom mouse that came over with glasses of water for all of them.

When they finally caught their breath again and took long drinks of their water, the little storyteller finally looked at Cara.

"Who's that?" he whispered to Woodrow, still keeping his eyes on Cara.

"That is my friend. Her name is Cara. She's helping me make my deliveries today."

Cara waved.

"I'm Zeke," he said, waving back slightly.

"Good to meet you, Zeke," she said and watched as he rolled to his side and put his head down.

Cara and Woodrow exchanged looks, but Cara saw in his eyes not to ask.

"I'm so glad you told me that story, Zeke. You'll tell me another one when I come back later this week, right?" Woodrow said.

Zeke just nodded and closed his eyes. In only a few moments, he was asleep and lightly snoring.

They got up and walked over to the doorway again.

"How's he doing, honestly?" Woodrow asked the mom.

"His energy is still low, as you can see. Little bursts here and there and it's gone. I'm not sure if he's getting much better. I've got the doctor coming today to see if he can do anything."

"Let me know what he says. I'll be back in a couple of days," Woodrow said, casting another look Zeke's way.

The mom threw her arms around Woodrow, holding him tight for a moment before opening the door and letting them say their goodbyes.

This time when Woodrow grabbed Cara's hand, she didn't fight. They shot back up to full size and Woodrow commanded the bag to follow them and they headed down the street again to another home.

"What's wrong with the little guy?" Cara finally asked before they stopped at the next place.

"Well, we're pretty sure he has cancer. We don't have too many tests that we can do, but that's what it looks like. We've been trying all sorts of different medications and we've got doctors around the clock trying to come up with new ones, but this is all new to us."

"You, you get cancer here?" Cara asked.

"You wouldn't believe what all we get here."

"But can't you just, I don't know, use magic to get rid of it? You use it for so many other things," she asked, bewildered.

"Not since Sarith and the beast showed up. That darkness changed everything."

Even your health, Cara thought as Woodrow knocked on the next door.

All day, they stopped at homes throughout the city. One by one, the animals thanked him for bringing them food. Woodrow explained that a lot of the caregivers couldn't leave the sick ones to get things, so others around the town stepped up to help them. Woodrow helped with food, while another did cleaning, and still another did visits.

"And you all take care of each other," she said, more to herself than to him.

"That's what friends do for each other," he said.

They came up to a hole in the ground that Cara initially thought was a tunnel entrance until Woodrow knocked loudly. Cynthia poked her head up and stopped midway out.

Cara looked down at her feet and let her toes dig into the dirt.

"I didn't know Cara would be joining you today, Woodrow," Cynthia said, moving to let them pass.

"How are you making out? Have some help today?" Woodrow asked and walked past the door she held open for them.

Cara dragged her feet as she walked past Cynthia and entered her home. The entryway was quite small, but once Cynthia led them into the living room, Cara was startled by how large it was. It almost felt like the dream-writing room, where it seemed so small at first, but once in there, it was actually huge. This world seemed to have that effect.

Further into the room, she heard little voices coming quietly at first, then louder as they came towards them. A fluffle of baby bunnies swirled around Cara, jumping and laughing. A male rabbit followed behind, looking a bit frazzled, but so happy.

"This is my husband, Tom," Cynthia said, introducing them.

"Well, it's nice to finally put a face to the name," he said, putting a firm paw on Cara's hand before following the bunnies around the room, shushing them.

Cara watched Cynthia and saw her instantly light up when she saw her babies come into the room. She was like someone else suddenly. One of the smallest ones came over to Cynthia and jumped into her outstretched arms.

"She was the runt of the litter," Cynthia said, noticing that Cara was watching her. She gave the little one a big hug and let her back down.

"She's sweet," Cara said.

The tension between them was so thick it could be cut with a knife. Cara knew she needed to say something and make things better. She needed a friend, and maybe, if she could make things right, Cynthia could be it.

"Do you have somewhere that we could sit and talk?" Cara asked.

"Sure, we can talk in my study."

Cynthia led her to the room. Bookcases covered the walls, full of leather-covered books. In the middle was a modest wood desk with a simple lamp and an open notebook.

"I like to write," she shrugged, noting Cara's reaction.

"Have you written much?"

"I've written two novels and a few collections of short stories. I do it when I get a chance. Since the kids came around, it's been harder, but I'm getting there on this novel. I'm hoping to finish it in the next couple of months. It's been a lot of late nights."

Cara nodded and took a seat at a couch in the corner.

"Listen," Cara said, "the other day when I walked out like that, I didn't mean to hurt you. I'm really sorry," Cara whispered, her voice caught on a lump in her throat.

"Did I do something wrong? I was just trying to be nice," Cynthia asked, holding her hands in her lap.

"Nothing, it's nothing."

"I know that it's something. Please tell me."

Cara dug her hands down into her lap and wrung them until they burned and were bright red. Telling anyone her feelings was always a struggle for her. Every time she had in the past, someone had always turned it back around onto her and somehow made her the bad guy. It was always the same. And yet, as she sat here, it occurred to her she had done the same thing to Cynthia. Cynthia had tried to do something nice and extend the hand of friendship, but Cara jumped on her and turned it around on her. It was just like the other girls in the past had done to her. When did she turn into that person?

"It's something from my past. Something you said brought it up."

Slowly, she told Cynthia everything: from Melissa and the announcements and how embarrassed she was, to the taunting, and finally how the Hammer had hit her. As she spoke, she felt like she was folding in on herself. She never truly realized how hurt she was until it all came pouring out. Tears and fears mixed and intertwined as she poured out her heart like never before. She couldn't stop the sobs that now came freely and quickly, like a train rushing out the station. She couldn't stop. It was turning into an ugly, blubbering cry and her body shook from the pain that now was finally leaving her.

Cynthia was stunned at first, but gently came over and gave her a hug. Cara shook it off initially, but Cynthia came back and hugged her firmer. Cara knew she wouldn't let go and if she was truly honest with herself, she didn't want her to. She let herself exhale and shrink into Cynthia's hold and felt the warmth and peace in her furry embrace.

When she finally caught her breath and released herself from the hug, she looked at Cynthia and suddenly saw she was larger than normal. She was now almost Cara's size when she normally was only a small rabbit.

"I have the gift of comfort," she smiled and patted Cara's shoulder. "I am not those girls, and I never will be. I am me. And I really like you. I will never initially hurt you."

"I know. Sometimes it's difficult to remember, though. Sometimes it's easier to assume the worst."

"Well, at least here, I want to be that person for you that you can turn to and get comfort from. Don't let your past experiences tarnish future relationships."

Cara sniffled, wiping her nose with the back of her hand. Cynthia led Cara out of the study and back to the other room. The baby bunnies were still running around and causing chaos, but Cynthia looked at them with a mother's warmth. Cara knew that look very well from her own mother.

"You know that little one that I mentioned earlier? The runt? Well, they didn't think she was going to make it for the first few days. Everyday we said a prayer and I kept her close and as warm as possible. And this little one was a fighter. She really surprised everyone." Cynthia said. She turned to Cara and looked her square in the eyes.

"Cara, be a fighter. Even if it's not for us."

Cara knew she meant more than just defeating Sarith. She meant even more than just the bullies at home. She knew in the core of her being that Cynthia meant for herself. Fight for her right to be happy and fight to be the person who she was always meant to be.

"I hate to cut this short, but we have a few more stops to make on the way home, unless you can sneak away and come with us?" Woodrow said, shooting Tom a sly smile.

"Have fun, honey," he said and waved her away.

Cynthia linked arms with Cara and led her out the door and down the street.

Twenty-Nine

As Cara and Cynthia walked ahead of Woodrow, Cara could already feel his sly smile from behind her. She turned a couple of times to catch it, but each time, he looked away quickly and focused on the remaining food in his bag.

They stopped at another few homes, most of which were sick and bedridden, but it was the final stop on their way that made Cara breakdown.

The home was small and in much need of repair. The stonework and mortar were crumbling around it. Ivy grew over some windows and the roof shingles were peeling up on the corners. Cynthia and Woodrow went right up to the door, about to knock, but Cara hung back. Who would live in such a horrible place? And why had no one done anything to help them?

Woodrow knocked. Cara could hear what sounded like a hollow echo coming back to them.

Slowly, the door creaked open to a deep darkness.

"I'm going to light a lantern," Woodrow said, stepping into the home and going for a counter just inside.

"Where are we?" Cara asked.

Cynthia held her finger up to her lips, and Cara hushed.

They walked into the home and the smell of something burning hit her. She held her hand up to her nose, trying not to breathe, but the smell was overpowering.

Further into the darkness where even the light of the door wouldn't touch, was an old couch stained colours she couldn't even decipher in this pale of light. They approached and saw an eagle, laying under a blanket that was curled up to his beak.

"We brought you some food." Woodrow held up the bag and the eagle nodded. "Would you like us to make you anything?"

The eagle shook its head and rolled to face them. Cynthia and Cara hung back.

"You don't have to keep checking on me," he said in a harsh whisper.

"I know you. Was today a good day?" Woodrow asked.

He shook his head again and rolled over to his other side and away from them all.

"We'll come again next week," Woodrow said, turning to Cynthia and Cara.

"If I make it that long," the eagle huffed.

As they walked out the door, Cara turned back and saw he still hadn't moved. She couldn't understand what was going on, but her heart was breaking seeing anyone live like that. Silent tears welled up in her eyes and she tried to swallow down her emotions, but the tears broke free, racing down her cheeks.

"What happened to him?" she asked, as Woodrow closed the door.

"He was one of the first to be attacked by Sarith. She hit him with a fireball so hard he never recovered. That fire stayed in him. He's dying, slowly being burned from the inside out. That's why he has the scent."

"Is there nothing the doctors can do for him?" Cara asked, whipping away a tear.

"No, they have tried, but it hasn't worked."

"Human magic?" Cara said, knowing it before she even said it.

"Yes."

"And that's another reason you wanted me to come today," Cara said.

"I wanted to show you we are good creatures. We have a lot of great things but we also have some genuine hurt and pain here too. Every day is a struggle for us, even though it looks like magic makes it easier.

"Before you truly decide to not help, I wanted you to know there are some here that are hurting and need someone to take care of them. We do what we can but sometimes even we can't do enough. But through it all, we try to help each other because that's what life is all about."

They walked through the town and back towards Woodrow's home. Cara was unsure what to say. As they approached, Woodrow stopped. Cara and Cynthia stopped ahead of him and turned.

"Actually, I need to clear my head. I'll meet you at the pub. I'm going to just walk around a bit," he said.

"Are you sure?" Cynthia asked.

"Yeah. I'll see you soon."

He walked away, shoulders down.

"Now what do we do?" Cara asked Cynthia, as they walked into Woodrow's home.

"Now, we eat."

Thirty

The sun was already setting as Cara and Cynthia left Woodrow's home. Across the way, the clock tower told them it was almost time to meet up with Woodrow. They crossed the street and headed towards the pub. Around her, the townsfolk were making their way home for the day. She still couldn't believe how many species could be together in harmony. Back in her world, this would never happen. She watched as they laughed together, hanging on each other's arms.

Slowly, Cara saw the magic happening. It was transforming everything. Someone across the road pointed up at each street light and it would light up. Another walked along and the flowers quickly folded up for the night. Still another raised his hands and his shop lights went out and the exterior door closed and locked.

She stopped and watched as small sparrows flew along and hung lines of small white lights overhead, giving the place a warm backyard feel. Cara couldn't deny the beauty of the place. The nearby mountain, the tall trees full of dark greens of every shade, felt just like her aunt's cottage back home. Her heart ached thinking about home. She missed it so much.

When they reached the pub, Cara pushed open the wooden door and stepped inside. The room was full. On one side sat deep circular booths with animals laughing and eating enormous plates of food, while on the other side of the room was the bar. Some animals stood at it, ready to place orders, but most stood off in the middle, holding drinks, talking loudly over the live band that played in the corner. Cara didn't recognize the song, but the beat was catchy and it made her want to dance.

The room was lit with the candle wall sconces that gave the room a warm, welcoming glow. As she stepped into the room, many of the animals stopped and looked at her, but she was getting used to that. Making her way through, she smiled politely while she looked for Woodrow. He was at the bar near the back.

"Cara!" Woodrow said, giving her a sloppy hug, and pointing to a nearby bar stool.

She couldn't help but laugh as she took a seat. Woodrow was barely recognizable as he laughed and talked loudly to those around him. She knew it was the drinks he had had, but even still, it was nice to this relaxed side.

"I ordered two champagnes. I know it's kind of an unusual choice, but I feel like celebrating. A human found our world!" Woodrow said.

Cara watched as the bartender reached for the bottle and without even touching it, it lifted and turned around.

The cork popped, two glasses floated over and rested gently on the bar and he filled them, bubbles growing to the top, hers spilling over. He wiped it down with a fresh towel before sliding them across the counter.

"So literally everything is done by magic," Cara said, shaking her head. Even after all these days of being here, she still couldn't wrap her head around it all.

"Well, there are things we do by hand, not because magic won't work, but because of the joy those things give. I love the feeling of dirt against my paws. Plus, there are things that physical touch does better. And really, anything to do with emotions and feeling can only happen through touch or interaction." Woodrow clinked their glasses together and took a drink.

"Magic lets us add to a lot, but it's not everything. And when it comes to the beast and the woman he works for... well, that's its own thing again. Our magic isn't strong enough for that. Even all combined. I think that's why so many had high hopes... Sorry, I'm just rambling now.

"Anywayssss, let's par-ta like we don't have a care in dez world. Hopefully James will have good news tomorrow," he said, slurring as he raised his glass again and they clinked once more.

Cara took a sip and looked around. The pub was full already. Everyone looked so happy. Most were in groups, laughing and joking around. The bubbles of the champagne tickled her nose. She felt the warmth of the drink already as it made its way into her. And yet, reality reared its ugly head again. Even though this single moment was calm and peaceful, it didn't mean it would stay this way.

Their world could come crashing down at any given moment. Cara downed the rest of her drink as Woodrow greeted another friend and left to walk around the room. It was only a few moments before a pair of cheetahs came over to her.

"Cara, I'm so glad you're here!" said the one on the right. Her almond-shaped eyes shone against her golden fur.

"Yeah! Thanks for being here," said the other.

Cara mumbled a 'you're welcome' to them before she took a few steps away. She had barely moved before three more animals came up and expressed their thanks. Over and over as she sipped on a fresh drink she was given, animals from all over the bar came over to talk, if only for a moment. Even just looking around, she had head nods and smiles all around her. She had never felt so conflicted. It was easy to leave when you didn't know the folks affected by it. But now, she saw the hope and joy in their eyes. They didn't know she wanted to leave. They didn't know she couldn't do magic. And they didn't know she wasn't the one they had hoped for all this time. But they did have hope. And as she watched them all, she wasn't sure how she would ever tell them otherwise.

Across the room, Cara watched as the pub door opened and James walked inside.

"James, you made it!" she said, as he came over to her and wrapped his arm around her. She laughed, not expecting that. His fur was frazzled and his clothes were askew.

"I got someone to cover my shift. I've spent no time with you really and I want to. When you two weren't at the house, I figured you'd be here. Everything else is closed up for the night."

"I'm glad to see you too," Woodrow said, but avoided looking him in the eye. James came around to him and grabbed his shoulders, rubbing them jokingly before giving him a playful shove.

Woodrow laughed. In that simple gesture, all was forgiven.

"The boss let you off work early?" Woodrow joked.

"I thought about what you said, Woodrow, and you're right. I do need a bit of time off to relax and enjoy," James said, taking a seat. "So I thought, why not come and spend some time with our famous visitor and get to know her better?"

"It's about time," Woodrow said, waving over a server.

"What can I get for you?" The server asked, leaning in to hear as the noise level in the bar continued to elevate.

"Another round of drinks! Champagne all around!" one of them shouted.

From across the bar, the twins spotted them and came over, raising a toast to Cara. She took another drink from the server and took another sip. Her head spun. The lights seemed brighter suddenly, and she couldn't think straight. She wasn't sure how many glasses of champagne she had had now, but it was all coming to her at once. It sent her thoughts and feelings soaring into the space. All around her, eyes sparkled and drifted back towards her. She could feel the electricity in the air as the hopes they all had seemed to hang there.

The twins shouted something into Woodrow's ear before waving at her and leaving the pub.

"They are going to start the fire now. We'll be able to head over there anytime," Woodrow said. He turned back towards James.

She had to admit, even just to herself, that this place was pretty incredible. And not just the pub, but the whole world. She watched as another group of friends made their way in. As the pub filled, the air got warmer and her head spun more. She needed some air.

"Fresh air," she shouted into James's ear, pointing to the door.

James nodded and led the way.

As they left, Cara turned for one last look around. The bliss these animals felt tonight and the hope they had hung in the air. She almost couldn't even bear it. And it was Woodrow's smile across the bar that really hit her the most. He had so much hope and even though she still doubted herself, he never did. She followed James outside to the cool air, their breaths coming out in white, misty clouds.

"It got really packed in there! I don't think I've ever seen it that busy before," James said.

"It's because of me. I'm the one that everyone wants to see, even if it's just a quick glance. James, I can't do this," she blurted out.

"Don't think about it now. Just let yourself have fun! Tonight, the beast is far away, Sarith is nowhere to be seen, and we have friends and drinks all around. Let's just have one fun night where we can burn off some energy. Let yourself relax."

Maybe he was right. Maybe for just one night, she should stop.

"When are we heading to the fire?" she asked.

"How about I go get Woodrow and we can go there now? The fresh air will be good for us all," James said as he disappeared inside and Cara let her eyes wander.

The cool night air felt good against her skin, and it was helping clear her head. The lights still hung overhead, twinkling like the stars above. Even in this darkness, she could still see the mountain high in the distance.

The door of the pub opened again, sending a beam of orange light into the darkness around her, the music now blaring loudly. Woodrow and James came around the door and hooked arms with her. Cara laughed, feeling like she was being lifted off the ground.

"It's like we're in the movie "Wizard of Oz." Arms linked and heading towards the wizard, hoping to be able to go home," Cara laughed.

They both looked at her confused and she realized they didn't know what she was talking about. They didn't have televisions here.

She shook her head and pulled her arms out, letting them swing beside her instead.

As they entered the woods, the air chilled more and she felt shivers go up her spine.

Woodrow stopped, his ears darting up. He held his arm up for her to stop. He sniffed the air. Cara, puzzled, tried to hear what he did but all she heard was silence. Not even the breeze blew through the trees.

"What is it?" she whispered.

He hushed her and waited. She couldn't hear anything. There wasn't a single sound to be heard, not even the crickets that had earlier been singing their song. It was quiet. Too quiet. She strained. Somewhere in the distance, the beast let out a bellow, only it didn't seem so far away now.

Cara's heart skipped a beat and she ducked low. Woodrow looked over and motioned for her to follow him.

"Woodrow, are we going to be okay?" she breathed.

They inched through the woods.

"I don't know."

James led the way now as Woodrow slipped in behind her. They were surrounding her.

"We need to get to that fire and get them out of there and back to town before something happens," James said, whispering into her ear. She could hear the quiver in his voice and the weight of the words hit her. Their friends were in danger. They needed to get them out of there now.

Thirty-One

They crept through the woods. Cara's heart knocked loudly and she was sure hers wasn't the only one. All around them, the forest remained strangely quiet. It was almost as though the trees were scared to make a sound in case they were found out.

"This way," Woodrow whispered, leading them to the right. Cara didn't know where they were going or how long it would take them to get there, but with every step, it became more difficult to move. She wanted to turn and run. She never went towards danger. Every instinct was telling her to run.

A laugh rang out from her right. She stopped to listen. Another laugh came and she heard someone shout something. The three of them pointed and swiftly made their way over to it. Through the fog that had formed emerged a bright yellow glow. It was like a ray of hope amongst the darkness she had felt like she was in. As they approached, Cara saw the flames of the campfire.

"I'm telling you, he did that the other night! I couldn't believe what I was seeing." They all laughed again. Cara scanned the group surrounding the fire and saw Michael and Anthony, faces light and glowing from the flames. They were laughing with three others she didn't know, all of them totally unaware of the impending danger.

She breathed a sigh of relief. They were okay. But the surrounding quiet continued. Maybe the drinks were playing games with their heads.

They crept up closer. Woodrow signalled for them to stop. Her body shook as the cold seeped into her body and bones.

Or was the shaking because of her fear? she wondered. She couldn't see the beast anywhere, but she knew it was somewhere close by. Woodrow and James both took a deep breath and nodded to each other. Woodrow held up a hand and counted to three. They took a step towards the fire but Cara couldn't move. Something didn't feel right. Suddenly, she felt warmth coming from somewhere. She couldn't be sure where. She went to stop them, but it was already too late.

* * *

It was swift. The growl was so close it pierced Cara's ears and rattled her whole body. The group around the campfire looked up, their faces instantly drained of colour. No one had heard the beast approach. A scream went up and suddenly it was chaos. The group scattered but the beast was too close. They ran. It burst through the trees, snapping branches and crushing them like twigs. It growled again, sending the earth shaking. Michael and Anthony looked up in horror but were frozen in place, just like she had that first day. She took a step forward to help but before she could make any distance, the beast swung its head down low and in a fluid motion grabbed both of the twins in its mouth. Cara met eyes with Michael and the look of fear in his eyes scared her to the bone. And in the next second, the beast bit down.

Cara heard their screams, then sudden silence as the sound of bones cracking echoed over to her. She turned away, holding her hand over her mouth. She didn't know if the beast would hear her being sick over the sound of bones popping, but either way, she didn't want to be next.

James stopped mid-step. Cara grabbed him and pulled him back. Woodrow was already stumbling backwards, colliding with them and sending them to the ground. Terror consumed their faces.

The beast howled again. Blood dripped from his teeth, hitting the ground below, soaking the grass with crimson.

Escape was impossible, but she could hide. Cara looked around and to her right, she saw a fallen log. Even in the dark light, she saw a hole at the one end.

She grabbed James's paw and pointed to the log. He nodded and grabbed Woodrow. They scrambled in and covered their ears. The earth shook as the beast was moving now. He was looking for others. He bellowed again, the tree shaking, but it didn't sound like he was coming any closer.

Cara looked at her friends. The only thing visible on their faces was fear etched deeply.

She could hear the beast breathing, the metallic smell of blood filling the air. She felt herself gag, but her stomach held. He snorted and huffed. Even at a distance, she could feel the heat radiating off him and his stench was sickening. Time slowed. She waited. She could feel her legs cramping. Pain radiated up and down her legs and in her feet. It began as a dull ache, but quickly grew until it was a deep throbbing that sent waves through her whole body. She bit her tongue. The pain was becoming too much. Just when she thought she couldn't hold on anymore, the beast sneezed. She shifted and stopped. Her friend's eyes grew enormous with panic. He sneezed a second time and repositioned himself. What felt like an eternity passed and yet the beast remained where he was, quiet and unmoving. She leaned over to James and cupped her hands around his ear.

"Do you think it's safe?" she asked.

He shrugged.

"I'm going to check," she said, unsure why she would volunteer for this, but they couldn't stay there forever.

She carefully pulled herself to the end of the log and she saw the beast was now laying on his side with his tongue hanging loosely out of his mouth. His eyes were closed and his breathing came in deep, slow motions. He was sleeping. She crept out and was hit by the smell of his breath. It was a mix of metal and rotting flesh. Between his teeth, she saw what was left of bones and tufts of fur. She turned away, partly to avoid the sight and smell, and partly to see if there was a way for her to get far away from him. She looked down into the log and motioned for them to follow but put her finger to her lips.

They crept out silently and stopped only a moment before James pointed to the pathway that had brought them from town. The beast remained still, sleep having claimed him after his meal. Once on the path and out of sight, they ran. They ran as fast as they could. Cara tried to only focus on the path. She couldn't see Woodrow or James through the thick vale of tears that were now streaming down her cheeks. The fog was thinning and out of it, the town emerged.

The little shops and homes never looked so good. Cara was happy to be back but terrified for all of them. Everything was dark. Not a single light was lit as they raced through the town. They must have heard the beast attack.

They didn't stop until they were back at Woodrow's home. They closed the door and all of them stood in stunned silence. Cara couldn't shake that final look of fear Michael had given her. It was a look that would haunt her forever. Even now, the sound of the popping bones was circling its way around and around in her head.

"What do we do?" Woodrow asked, leaning against the edge of the dining room table.

"What can we do?" James said. "We know she is stronger. We know we can't do anything to defend ourselves. Even if we had thought to use magic back there, it would have been useless."

"We're going to have to go into hiding. That was too close to town. We're in danger here," Woodrow said.

"We can't just leave our home. In the morning, we'll gather everyone and see if there's a way to fight. We have to at least try to stand up for ourselves," James said.

"I'm sorry, but did you not just see what we saw?" Woodrow said, gesturing the way they had come.

"I know. But we have to try!" James said. "We need to tell the mayor, and I think maybe I should be the one to tell him."

"I don't think I can," Woodrow exclaimed. "This is all so horrible." He got up and paced the room, before quickly sitting back down and grabbing his stomach. He leaned forward, putting his head between his knees, and took a few deep breaths.

"Woodrow, it's okay. I'm used to horrible things, although they are usually written, but I feel like I see them when I see those animals writing them."

"Cara, I don't know what kind of impression you are getting of our town, but it's never been like this before. Ever. Things are definitely getting worse," Woodrow said.

"That might be the case, but we don't need to worry Cara about all this. I know things aren't great right now," James said, holding up his palm to Woodrow who looked ready to interrupt, "but we need to keep just pressing on and knowing that in the end things will work out. It has to.

"I'll be back shortly. I'm going to talk to the mayor and we should have a service ready for tomorrow sometime," he said, looking at the clock. It read after midnight. "Or I should say, later today. I'll let you know what's decided. Cara, keep an eye on him. When he gets this upset, he loses all sense of everything," James said, shooting his friend a look out of the corner of his eye as he walked out the door.

Cara locked the door behind James. She couldn't believe he was leaving again. Now, more than ever, they needed to stay together and figure this out. She walked over to Woodrow and put her hand on his shoulder. He stood and excused himself to his room. Cara watched him go and retreated to her own room. Maybe in the light of day, things would be easier.

Thirty-Two

The beast came roaring back to the castle as Sarith found her way to the backfield that rested behind it. She felt him coming as he shook the ground around her.

She let out a low whistle and felt the air shift as the beast turned and headed towards her. After all these years, she still wasn't used to the smell that came off of him. It was so strong she knew when it was coming even before she felt the ground shake.

As he came over to her, she could still see the bloodstains on his fur.

"You were successful, I assume," she said, sizing him up.

"The twins are gone," the beast roared, breathing out deeply, flushing her with heat from his sour breath.

She coughed, then straightened herself. Slowly, a laugh escaped her lips.

"Was she there?" Sarith asked, a hint of hope in her voice.

"She was. So were Woodrow and James. They hid, but I saw them."

"Very good. Maybe that will finally light a fire under her."

"Well, if this doesn't, I'm not sure what will," the beast replied, scratching his ear with his back foot.

"For now, you leave them alone. Let's see what this woman is really about. I'll tell you what's next when the time comes. I will send the General to find out if we have scared her straight or not yet."

Sarith watched as the beast disappeared back to its cave, she assumed, and walked around to the training field. She couldn't wait to see what Cara would do next.

Thirty-Three

The morning was a quiet one. Neither Woodrow nor Cara felt much like talking. Woodrow made them breakfast, then excused himself again and went out to the garden. Cara figured it was to clear his head. She stayed nearby and watched him work. Even bent down, digging in the dirt, he still looked defeated and hurt. His shoulders seemed to hang impossibly low, and she wished there was something she could do for him.

James arrived for lunch, but no one ate. Later, they walked together through the town and towards the church. The townsfolk were already gathering, most with handkerchiefs in hand, dabbing moist eyes. They greeted each other with solemn voices.

Cara had only been to one funeral her whole life; her grandfather's. She was eleven years old when he died and it had hit her hard. Maybe because it was the only day she had ever seen her own father cry. Seeing the tears falling down the cheeks of a strong and confident man was almost too much to bear. Walking into the church that day and seeing the one she loved laying there in a perfect-looking casket but at the same time, looking nothing like they used to, was incredibly difficult to handle.

She still remembered the high sheen of the wood and the almost blinding brightness of the brass accents. It all looked so perfect and cold. Her grandfather wasn't this type of fancy guy. He was a simple man who had well-loved furniture in his home and a caring and open heart. This wasn't like him at all and the stark contrast of it all sent her spiralling emotionally. Cara had hugged her father and held his hand through the service, but she knew there was no way to comfort him. He walked with his head high and his shoulders back, trying to put on a brave face, but the pain was etched in the frown lines on his face. She tried to keep it together like he had tried, but she couldn't. The tears had flowed like rivers down her face and spilling onto her lap.

As she walked into the church today, the sight of the mourning animals had brought it all back to her. She swallowed against the lump in her throat and forced her suddenly heavy feet to walk down the pew and sit, waiting for the service to begin.

Woodrow looked at her with a strained smile. Over the last few hours, she had seen the weight of it all taking its toll. Even through the fur surrounding his eyes, she could make out the dark, heavy bags.

"I know you didn't know them well, but thank you for coming," he said.

Cara gave him a polite smile before turning to watch as Terrance walked up to the podium and cleared his throat.

"Thank you all for coming," he began.

* * *

The service wasn't long. She could see how everyone tried to just keep themselves together, most on the verge of tears. As the animals around her shared stories about Michael and Anthony and what they meant to everyone, she could see why they were so special to them.

They had been the first set of twins to survive in this world. They were the only children to the one town founder too. Initially, many thought they would end up on the wrong side of things. They were always causing trouble, sometimes with practical jokes or pranks, but at other times, breaking the law. But one of the town elders had taken them under his wing and help them turn themselves around. From then on, they not only became favourites around the town, but they also contributed a lot. They became town council members, volunteered to help those that were sick, and even began teaching at the community centre. They had been taken far too soon. There was so much more they could have done if only they had had the chance.

After the service, Woodrow, Cara, and James made their way down to the chapel, where everyone piled in and held plates of finger foods that mostly remained untouched.

Cara felt so out of place, but everyone that approached them shared sympathy with her, too.

"Woodrow?" she asked, motioning him off to the side of the room.

He looked around and joined her.

"These two were pretty special," she said, not sure how to continue her thoughts.

"Yeah, they really were."

Silence fell between them just as a server came by with a tray of finger foods. They both shook their heads, and he continued to the next in the room.

"Do you do this kind of service every time someone passes because of the beast?" She stopped looking around and finally met his eye-line.

"This is the first time we've had an attack like this. Most of the time, they either get away scared, or they are taken. We've never seen anything like this before."

"How is that possible?" she asked, shocked.

"Honestly, I don't know. I guess you could say we've been fortunate that way," Woodrow said, nodding at someone as they went by.

"But, but-, that thing has been attacking you all so often."

"I know," he replied, gently nodding to a friend across the room.

"So, me being here has made this thing change and now it wants to attack, or at least is attacking now."

"Yeah, I guess so." He let his voice trail off, but she knew that neither of them was buying it.

"What are you two talking about now?" James said, so close to Cara she jumped.

"I didn't even hear you walk up," she said, turning towards him and moving so he could join the conversation.

"We're just discussing the twins and our current situation," Woodrow replied.

"The beast is getting more violent now," James said, looking at a faux-bacon wrapped water chestnut before popping it in his mouth.

"How can you be so calm about this?" Woodrow asked, watching him eating.

"Don't get me wrong, it's awful and I'm definitely upset about it, but surely you knew things were going to change. The beast is getting closer and we have no idea how to stop it from attacking us. Unfortunately, this is what I figured would happen sooner or later. I'm just waiting for the day that we all have to go into hiding, and I don't mean just in a small town where he can't find us. I mean having to hide underground and away from everything we've ever known."

Woodrow watched his friend say all this as calm as ever, like he was talking about the weather and shook his head.

"And you're just prepared to sit back and let this happen?" Woodrow said, scratching his head between his ears.

"Of course not!" James replied. "I'm going to put away supplies before it's too late, and I'm going to tell everyone else to do the same. I think we need to do a test on that lake and see if there really is a way we can get Cara home before she gets too wrapped up in all of this and gets hurt."

"But," Woodrow stuttered over the words. A server holding glasses of wine walked past, and he grabbed two glasses. Cara reached out for one, but Woodrow hadn't seen. He lifted the first to his lips and downed it in a single gulp, and immediately started sipping on the second one.

"You can't just give up!" Cara said, looking back and forth between them.

"Cara, we can't stop Sarith. Humans have stronger magic than anyone or anything else here, even all of us combined. Unless we take measures to protect ourselves now and go into hiding, our society is doomed.

"I know when I saw you that first day, I thought maybe you could be the one to do it, but I can see that it isn't something you want to do and don't feel you can do. So now we need to be realistic and do what we have to for ourselves," James said, shifting his weight and looking around.

"I can't defeat her." She crossed her arms and could feel her fears rising again.

"I know you can't," James said, wiping his mouth and fingers on a napkin before tossing it in a nearby garbage can. "I'm not asking you to anymore."

James turned to leave them both standing there stunned, but Cara quickly grabbed his shoulders and turned him back towards them.

"I can't let you all die," she said.

"But what can you do? Being here, seeing this service and knowing that you can't help has really brought things into perspective for me. I know now that we just need to prepare for the future and, in the meantime, figure out a way that you can get home."

"I could try," she whispered.

She was met with silence. The words hung in the air like thick clouds, ready to start a storm.

"Oh?" He asked, meeting her eyes.

"Yes. I can't guarantee that I'm going to manage it, but I can't let a whole community die because I'm too scared to try!"

She knew there was a better chance of her failing, maybe even dying in the process, but if she didn't try, then where would she be? Once again, she'd be the scared little girl again, hiding in the stairwell of the high school. She'd be the one who pretended to be busy with homework or something else, while trying to hide from the bullies who might find her there.

Isn't that what bullies always wanted anyway? she thought as she looked into their faces. They always want to just keep you down. They don't want you to rise to the occasion and attempt to be stronger and better. And they definitely don't want you to realize you are stronger than they made you believe. No, they want to keep you low so they feel better in their own minds. She wasn't sure what led bullies to that point, yet she had witnessed it repeatedly with girls from her school, and now Sarith was doing the same thing. It wasn't okay. She would not let it happen anymore. Cara was going to stand up to her. Now was the time to be strong.

Woodrow stepped up beside James and ducked his head into her eyesight.

"You're going to try?" Woodrow asked, his tail bouncing in hope.

She raised her head and met their eyes. And for the first time, the thought of battle didn't scare her, instead she felt a wave of confidence rush over her. It was so unfamiliar but felt so good.

"I have to."

Thirty-Four

Woodrow grabbed her hand and led her out to an open field just past the lake. It was full of tall grasses and wildflowers, all dancing in the warm spring breeze. All around the field was a forest, except on the far side, that seemed to suddenly disappear.

"We're going to stay over to this side. That's a cliff," Woodrow said, pointing to their far left. "It probably drops a good thirty feet."

Cara looked, but followed him to the far side of the field where James stood waiting. She let her fingers dance across the tops of all the plants, most of which she had never seen before. This world had so many unique things already. Why not plants too, she figured.

From behind them, they heard someone call James's name. They turned and saw a camel standing there, looking uncomfortable.

James turned back to the two of them and shrugged. "I guess I'll have to catch up with you both later."

He turned and left them standing there, both bewildered.

"How does he have things to do right now?" she said. "He was the one that wanted to see me trying the most."

"Honestly, I don't know. Only thing I can figure is Sarith and the dreams are more demanding these days."

"I guess so," she said.

"Okay, we'll start small."

Woodrow signalled for her to stay where she was as he walked further out into the field. As he went, he let his fingers dance over the tops too and she noticed they started to shift and move.

"Magic isn't something you have to be scared of. It's actually quite a beautiful thing when you give it a chance," he said.

Cara watched as the grasses continued to dance and move and slowly from deep below, she could see a small tree trunk emerge. It kept growing until it was taller than either of them. Cara ran over to him, but still kept her distance. She could see Woodrow was enjoying this.

"We are always learning more and more about magic. Every day, there seems to be something new. You don't need to be afraid."

He continued holding his hand out towards the swirling shape. It grew taller, and bright green leaves sprung out of the branches that stretched from it. The tree filled out, and it transformed first into a large oval, but quickly she saw a face emerge, followed by wings. It turned its head and she saw it was an eagle staring back at her. Its beak pointed right at her and its claws looked sharp and hooked. She rubbed her eyes, not believing the sight in front of her. The detail was impeccable. Every point on its wings, all made with leaves so green, they almost didn't appear real.

"How?" she squeaked out.

The eagle blinked and smoothly moved its head towards her. It pushed her with its beak and she stumbled back, laughing.

"Incredible," she whispered.

"That's the great part about magic. It can do more than you probably would ever expect."

"Like help me stand up to a bully?"

"Like stand up to a bully," Woodrow said, agreeing with her, his fluffy grey tail twitching in excitement.

Cara moved in towards it. Everything from the claws to the eyes, and the wings, were absolutely flawless. It mimicked her head movements as she turned this way and that, trying to take it all in. It opened and closed its mouth as though testing to make sure it worked and flapped its wings, causing it to break free from the trunk it was attached to. It flew up into the air; the movement causing her hair to fly up around her head and into her eyes. When her hair finally fell back down, she saw the eagle was now above her, circling them.

"Unbelievable," she laughed.

And then, in a blink, he took off. He was heading away from them and towards the mountain.

"What now?" she asked, watching until he disappeared around the mountain peak.

"Now he will enjoy his life. And with the change of the season, so will his time come to say goodbye. It's part of how things work here."

Cara couldn't wrap her mind around it. It seemed like too much. But yet, she saw it with her own eyes. It was real and it was there.

"Do you want to know more?" Woodrow asked.

"Absolutely," she said, excited to start.

Thirty-Five

"We all have magic here, even if it's just a little bit," Woodrow explained, as Cara ran her fingers through the grass around them. "We all have jobs we use our magic towards. James's magic works with paper. He can transport it, change it, and seal words on it, which is why he is in charge of the dream-writing room. I mostly use mine for gardening," he paused.

Cara looked up and saw him watching her, his eyes sparkling.

"Let's say I do have magic. How would I even try?" Cara asked. The moment of defeat she had encountered while trying on her own before came back, but she pushed it back down. Now was the time for confidence.

"Well, it shows itself in many ways. Sometimes small, sometimes large. What's one of your favourite things?"

"I love writing and photography... and hiking through the outdoors... I don't know."

"Well, we're outdoors. Let's start there. First, think about what you love about it. Think about how it makes you feel. Think about how it makes you come alive and makes everything else, all the struggles and drama in your life, seem, well, less terrible. And while you're thinking about that, hold your hand out and picture what you want to see happen. You want to create an eagle? Picture every part of it. Completely rebuild it, and it will appear in front of you."

"Okay," Cara said hesitantly. Cara shook out her shoulders, took a deep breath and closed her eyes.

She let her mind drift back to the last time she went out to take photographs. It had been at her last home and it was days before the move. She wanted to capture those last few things she had put off for years and taken for granted. One of those places was an old, burned-out shell of a home on the edge of town.

The home had burnt down years before, for reasons the fire department never figured out. It sat on a huge property as a sole reminder of the devastation that had happened that night. The walls, windows, and doors all remained, but the roof was mostly gone. All that remained were ragged, black jutted rafters, each one coming to a point over the open hole of a home. The image haunted her dreams, but she had seen something coming out of the rubble one day, and it had made her curious. As she walked up to the home, Cara carefully opened a door and stepped inside. Everything was destroyed either from the fire; the rains that soaked things repeatedly; or from looters trying to salvage something. But in the far corner, where a hole had been made by some loose bricks, she saw a family of cats huddled together. It was a mother with a litter of six kittens. They were so small she couldn't believe they had survived. The mother lay on her side as the kittens drank from her and she looked up with piercing blue eyes that almost pleaded for help. Cara went into the backyard and found a crate and put them all in it, before carefully bringing them home.

Although the kittens took a bit to put on weight, they were very friendly. The mother, however, was much more guarded, and wouldn't let Cara put her hands anywhere near her. Cara could tell she was wounded and scared, and very protective, like a momma bear. She wouldn't let Cara take her kittens anywhere out of her sight, so Cara learnt to do all the nursing and bathing while mom could watch.

As the weeks went on, the kittens got old enough and strong enough to be placed in homes. The night before the families were coming to pick up the kittens, she had one final moment with them. The mother cat came over to her and carefully curled up on Cara's lap and fell asleep. One by one, the kittens came over and slept with her. She could barely keep her emotions together as they stayed there until morning when the new owners came to pick them up.

She pictured that cat, the nervous momma cat, and tried to imagine creating another just like her. Holding out her hand, she let her mind focus on the size, shape, and being of that cat. She could see the fur, soft as a rabbit's, and those happy blue eyes after the mother had finally trusted her. She pictured it and focused on it as intensely as she could.

"Cara?" Woodrow asked, interrupting her thoughts.

She looked in front of her and saw that nothing had formed. She felt her shoulders slump.

"It's okay. Take another breath and try again. Maybe don't focus on making something, but instead think about the things in nature that you love," he suggested.

She could see the tall grasses swaying and dancing around her and through the open field. The sun shone down, kissing it with bright light and deep warmth. Chipmunks and sweet little mice scurried across the field and came up to her, looking up at her with eyes that were wide and questioning but quickly moving on when they saw she had nothing to give them. She lost herself in the moment, feeling and experiencing peace, and for even that brief second, she forgot everything else. No longer was she scared of the danger coming her way. No longer was she a loser, like the girls at school said. She was just her and there was only that. Her body relaxed, and the tension in her shoulders melted away. She stayed that way for some time before finally opening her eyes.

"Did I do it?"

Woodrow gently shook his head.

"You did so well. Even though you haven't created anything yet, you are tapping into that place in your mind and heart that you need to so you can create something."

"I really thought I would have had it. What am I doing wrong?" she asked, searching his eyes for answers.

"Nothing. We might be trying to do too much too quickly, or we might just need to try it a little differently."

"Seriously?" Cara said, the spell breaking. "That beast is closing in and we are all so close to getting hurt or worse, like dying. I have to have magic or what are we going to do?"

"You have to keep trying. No one becomes good at something after the first couple of tries. You have to try over and over again."

"I have been! Since that night I went to the lake by myself. I didn't have any more matches, so I tried to light the fire myself. It didn't work. I have nothing else to do so why not? But honestly, why should I think I have something special like the ability of magic? I'm just some dorky kid. Trust me, I know. I get told that every day at school. Melissa has made damn sure that I know I'm not special."

"Those are lies!"

She just shook her head and headed the way they came.

"Even after all you just saw now? You still don't believe? You need to actually believe in yourself. Did you know they thought I didn't have magic either at one time?" Woodrow said, letting his white and grey paws fall to his sides.

Cara stopped but didn't turn to look at him.

"When I was young, it took me much longer for my magic to show up. My parents and most of the townsfolk didn't think I had any for the longest time. They thought I might be the first animal here ever that would be without it. If anything, that would make me a loser. I went years without any real powers. It didn't seem to matter what I tried. But once I was old enough, I tried on my own, away from everyone's watchful eyes. And not just once or twice, but repeatedly. And eventually I found out that I had magic after all. For me it took when I was so happy that I just let go. I released everything: all my fears, worries and anxieties. I was free, if only for a moment. That's when things showed up. That's when I finally saw myself making something magical. I made a potted plant grow."

Cara slowly turned back towards him.

"Please don't go. I truly believe you can do this. You were brought here for a reason," he said.

Woodrow suddenly stopped and held up a hand. She paused but looked at him strangely.

"What?" she whispered, looking around.

Woodrow sank below the grass-line and put his ear to the ground. Cara didn't even have to do the same before she knew what he was hearing. The sound of the grass being stomped down came to her clearly.

She spun, her eyes darting each way, trying to find the source.

General Barabus emerged from the horizon and stopped. His eyes grew when he saw her. Woodrow stood facing her and turned slowly to see the General there, looking at them both. His lips curled into a chilling grin as he took a step towards them.

"What do we do?" Cara whispered.

"Run!"

Woodrow and Cara ran as fast as they could muster. The flowers that had been so beautiful before now whipped them in the face, stinging with each hit.

She glanced back and saw he was gaining on them.

Woodrow looked back, saw it, and stopped. She collided with him and they went spinning. They lay in the grass for only a moment, but he looked at her, his eyes filled with fear.

"Now would be the perfect time to believe in yourself."

He jumped to his feet and put his hands out in front of him. Slowly, a black cloud rose from the ground. At first Cara thought it was insects, but as she watched, she saw seeds of nearby flowers, along with wood chips and stones, all flew from the ground. It came together between them and General Barabus. It took her only a minute to understand what he was doing. He was building a shield to protect them. The General laughed and raised his hands up too. Slowly, a hole appeared in the middle of it, small at first, but Cara saw it only grew bigger and bigger. From the centre, she could see through to the other side that the General was laughing at them.

"That all you got?" he snarled.

Woodrow added more and more seeds and flowers. The cloud grew bigger and denser, but above the rushing sound of the seeds moving, they could make out the General's laugh. It grew louder as she saw the hole appear again, and the seeds and stones were being pushed away. The cloud shook, then everything went flying away. Woodrow took a deep breath and frantically looked around and saw the nearby trees of the forest. Cara watched as a branch from one of the outer trees on the right of them grew outwards towards the field and came out heading straight to him. It hit the ground, shaking the earth, then rose again on its way over to the General before it finally reached him. A tree on the left side of the field did the same. Woodrow turned back to the General, and she watched as it grew up over him and slowly came down, circling his entire frame.

Cara gasped but Woodrow stayed focused. She turned, her whole body cringing and waiting to hear him scream out in pain but there was nothing.

"Woodrow?"

"It's to trap him," Woodrow said, his arms twitching as he held them out.

The branches were now completely around him, his head vanishing from sight. In only a few moments, it all looked like just a mess of branches, all intertwined and locked together. Eventually, everything stopped moving and Cara and Woodrow looked at each other.

"Let's get out of here before he bursts his way through," Woodrow said, turning away from the General.

Cara grabbed his hand and ran.

From behind them, they heard creaking and crackling as branches were breaking and crashing to the ground.

"Woodrow!" Cara shrieked, looking back. General Barabus burst through, sending branches flying. Woodrow turned to look and lost his footing. He fell, his feet tripping over the uneven ground.

He let out a cry and she spun back to look at him. He was down.

"Go!" he shouted, but she darted over to help him up.

"I'm fine. I'm fine. Run!"

But now the General was only twenty feet away.

She helped him to his feet and turned to General Barabus. Fear raced through her and she squeezed his hand tight, ready to run. An electric pulse radiated out of them and hit the General, causing him to stumble.

"What?" Cara asked, but before Woodrow could say anything, she saw movement in the tall grasses around them. The sound of rushing footsteps came up quick and, at first, brought fear into Cara until finally she saw the source of the sound. Animals of all kinds came out and circled them, blocking them from the General and standing firm.

"What the—" the General said, stunned by the pulse. Then, he looked at the wall of creatures and chuckled.

"Oh, that's rich. You think that will really stop me?"

Cara looked at Woodrow again. Her heart raced. The animals around them stood tall and waited for the moment to attack.

"You simple creatures. When will you ever learn?" He crouched down for a moment before jumping high in the air and soaring over the protected line the animals had made. He landed right in front of Cara. Everyone turned.

"You," he said, pointing to her. "You are coming with me."

He took a firm hold of her wrist. Cara pulled hard to free herself but she was no match for him.

"I'm not going anywhere with you," she exclaimed, and he laughed once more.

"Think again," he hissed, crouching down to take off once again.

This can't be how this ends, Cara thought, *I'm stronger than this.* Anger washed over her and consumed her very core. Her ears grew hot, and she felt the heat of anger flare up in her. She grabbed his arm and with what she could muster, she tried to push him off, then let out a sound she had never heard herself do before. The General shrieked and suddenly his hand was gone. He grasped it with the other hand and looked at it in agony.

Then his eyes met hers. She was looking at him, stunned. Turning her hand over, she saw a whisper of smoke rising from her skin. The smell of hot fur rose to her nose. She looked at his clutched arm. The fur was gone and only fire-kissed skin remained.

What was once chaos around her now was silent.

"You burnt me," the General finally choked out the words. "You burnt me?"

"I uh, I," Cara stuttered.

"You have..." General Barabus whispered, a wicked grin spread across his face.

He turned. Cara took her stance. His hands were moving. She spun to look at her friends. Each one held firm in their stance, then without warning, were flung away one by one. Some turned to run, but General Barabus's magic was too fast. He lifted them up and sent them flying, so all who was left was Woodrow.

"Sarith will be very pleased to know you now have magic!" He grabbed her again, only this time by the waist. She struggled. She caught Woodrow's eyes. He was trying something, but she didn't know what and it wasn't working. She turned to the General and grabbed him by the shoulders. Anger raged in her, and her skin boiled. She put her hands on his chest and pushed as hard as she could. For a moment he remained in front of her, then suddenly he let out a shriek as he flew backwards. He smashed into the ground, skidding backwards twenty feet and squealed in pain. He rolled back and forth on the ground, quickly extinguishing the sparks of fire that had just started in his fur.

"Cara, we have to get out of here," Woodrow said. She couldn't move.

"Now!" he yelled, and she spun her head towards him.

He motioned for her to follow, and she finally felt her legs cooperate. She ran and he fell in line with her.

"I know somewhere we can go!" He pointed to his right but Cara saw nothing. They turned, running as fast as they could. Cara heard the heavy breathing of the General behind. He was already catching up. Woodrow came up behind her and shoved her. She fell below the soil line, crashing onto the floor of an underground tunnel. Woodrow came down and fell on top of her.

"He doesn't know the entrance to the tunnel," Woodrow said, as Cara stood and moved back towards the wall. She fell back against it and slid down until she was sitting.

"Just you wait," they heard the General say from over-head, "Tomorrow, at the lake. Midday. We attack!"

They both looked up, holding their breath, waiting to hear him come crashing through the ground too, but then all they heard was silence.

When they finally agreed that they were safe, Woodrow turned to her.

"You have magic after all," he said, a smile breaking across his lips.

Cara looked at him sheepishly. She was just as stunned as he was. She had never been that angry before, or at least she never let herself get that angry. But if she was truly honest with herself, it felt good. Not just to get angry, but to actually stand up for herself. She felt stronger than she ever had before.

"For you, you needed to get angry. You just had to harness that energy," Woodrow said, trying to hide his excitement, but his fluffy tail gave him away as it bounced around.

"I can definitely do that. I have a lot of that to work with," she replied.

"We need to get you back to town," Woodrow said.

"Wait. What happened when I grabbed your hand earlier? There was some kind of pulse or something."

"Honestly, I don't know. I've never seen that happen before. We need to get back somewhere safe though and hone this magic. Cara, you can help us defeat Sarith!"

Cara stood and brushed herself off. He was right. She could help them.

Now it was the time to fight.

Thirty-Six

She has magic! General Barabus thought as he ran through the forest. He couldn't wait to tell Sarith. He knew she would be pleased. Maybe this would mean good things to come for him in the future. But for now, they were going to have a battle on their hands.

The General rushed into the courtyard of the castle and headed to his training grounds. Some troops were going through the daily drills, while others stopped for some lunch. They quickly stood and saluted upon seeing him. A few looked at him with questioning looks as they saw the burn marks on his arms and chest, but he refused to acknowledge it. Instead, he half-heartedly returned the salutes as he continued into the castle. He stopped briefly in his room and threw on a fresh shirt before he continued on. He had to find Sarith first before he could tell the troops and he needed to tell them as soon as possible.

"Good day General Barabus," one guard said to him as he headed towards Sarith's room.

"Hello," he said, barely even slowly down.

"She's not in her room, if that's who you are looking for."

"Oh?" The General said, stopping before the door.

"She's practicing archery in the back."

Barabus gave a quick nod before turning back outside towards the back of the castle yard. In the distance, he could see her slender frame holding up a bow, eyeing the target she had her eyes set on.

He slowed as he neared, unsure what she was aiming for, but waited as she finally took her shot. He heard the impact as it hit a painted wooden target. The arrow sunk down deep, dead centre. Sarith let out a laugh and walked towards it.

"Ma'am?" He said, walking up behind her.

"What," she said, more as a statement than a question.

Sarith always hated being interrupted. Every time she was in the calm place of concentration, she was always being interrupted by these animals. She would have to appoint a number two to take off some of the pressure but she wasn't sure who she could fully trust. These animals still showed they only truly trusted each other.

"She has magic." The General opened up the shirt, exposing the burned flesh and the singed fur. The smell still hit him even after the run back here.

Sarith froze for a moment, stunned, and walked over. She held out her hand as if to touch and quickly pulled it back. Those were clearly the hands of a human. She had no question about that.

"Oh," she whispered. "How did this happen?"

"I found her and Woodrow out in a field close to the lake. That Woodrow character was showing her some things, but she was clearly clueless until I showed up. She got so mad at me she blew her lid and, well, you can see the rest."

Sarith rubbed her hands together, pleased. Finally, she would have a worthy opponent.

"So she does have magic after all."

"And from the little that I saw, it's strong. She wasn't expecting to have any. I could tell by her reaction. We need to prepare the army. I did as you said and told them we would attack tomorrow."

"Yes, yes it is." Sarith finally pulled her eyes away from the burn marks on his chest and walked over to the target. She pulled the arrow out and put it back into her quiver. "Tell the army."

"Yes ma'am. What do I tell them about her?" the General asked.

"Nothing other than that she is mine. No one is to touch her. I will deal with her myself."

"Yes ma'am."

Sarith walked past him and towards the castle. She didn't know if that other woman would be ready, but she definitely was going to be.

Thirty-Seven

Sarith walked into her bedroom and through to the closet. She entered it, but didn't bother looking at anything. Instead, she headed towards the back and on the furthest wall was a door. Knocking near the top of it made it pop open. Inside, she pulled at the string that hung in the middle. A single bulb lit up and she let her eyes adjust to the light before stepping in. The walls of the small room were lined with everything she would need for this battle: shields, armour, bows and arrows, and swords. She looked at the swords and grabbed her favourite. She had gotten some of her soldiers to make her multiple options, but one of them, a zebra named Bartholomew, had taken extra time and care to make something special. Although not enchanted, this sword was solid. She had sliced through many coconuts with very little effort. It even cut through bones like butter. She didn't know what it was about the metal that he had used, but it was the sharpest and most lethal of them all.

Sarith grabbed armour and a shield and walked back out of her room, through the castle, and out to the courtyard. General Barabus was already shouting orders and the army was assembling and putting on their armour.

"I want all of you to get used to the weight of this armour. You will not be taking it off until after battle. We attack tomorrow midday and we are going to win. Some of you may fall during this battle, but know that it will be for the greater good so that our queen, Sarith, may take over this land and she will rule with her firm hand."

A cheer went up and Sarith was pleased. So many of the army had been difficult to convince, but after a while they all gave in and decided that fighting with her was better than trying to stand up to her.

Sarith put on her armour and called out orders for the exercises to start. The clanging of metal swords was loud, but she relished the sound.

Sarith was ready. She had been ready for this day since she first came into this world. She knew someday someone would come and stand up to her, but she didn't expect someone so young. That would just make it easier. She laughed at how quickly she could picture this girl falling from her sword. And she would savour that moment for years to come.

Pulling out her bow and arrow, she aimed and watched as it hit a wooden fence across the courtyard. She lined up another shot and sliced the first arrow in half. She did that again and again, then switched over to magic. Creating a large fireball in her hands, she shot it at the arrows, the whole thing bursting into flames.

She knew she was ready. She had been preparing for this day for as long as she had been here. And when that girl came to the field tomorrow, she was going to crush her into the ground and leave no remains behind.

Thirty-Eight

Tucked amongst the trees surrounding the lake, Cara and her friends stood ready. Each was suited up with armour, swords and shields in hand, waiting for the right moment. She could feel the energy in the air as they shuffled and waited for Sarith to arrive. It was electric.

After leaving the field the previous day, they had rushed back into town and found Terrance in the city square, watching the fountain. He had appeared so defeated and hopeless, but upon hearing everything, his demeanour had changed. The rest of the afternoon was spent training, both out in the field and around the town; however, even that hadn't been easy. She quickly learnt that anger was the driving force behind her magic, but being angry for too long was exhausting. They had worked as much as they could through the night, but she crashed around one in the morning and dreamt nightmares worse than she had ever before. Sarith was not going easy on her. Cara woke up hours later in a cold sweat from a dream that rattled her to the very core. The images quickly faded but the feeling they gave her remained. Doubt was trying to settle in, but she pushed it away.

Holding her sword against her chest, she sucked in a deep breath and looked down the line of friends beside her. They were ready. She signalled for them to hold their positions, first down her left, then down her right, and she got the nod back.

In the distance, the lake glimmered in the sunlight, but there wasn't a soul around. The fish that had met their end there had been fully cleaned up. The quiet was almost eerie. Cara felt the adrenaline coursing through her body.

It began with barely a sound. The ground slowly shook. The noise got louder until it was almost deafening. She watched as the tops of the soldiers came over the hill beyond the lake.

They came like a wall made of shields and swords, walking together. Slowly, they filled the area around the lake. She watched as they all came to a stop together and waited. General Barabus came to the front and looked around. He spotted Cara instantly and they locked eyes. He gave her a look, trying to intimidate her, but she knew that this was what they had been preparing for, and he wouldn't get the best of her. Sarith wasn't anywhere to be seen.

Cara signalled for her friends to hold. She waited to see if Sarith would come to the front, but she didn't. She would be near the back, surrounded and protected. Cara laughed and shook her head. Of course, she was playing it safe. Cara drove her sword up in the air and the troops charged.

The armies came together like two crashing waves. The sound of clanging metal as swords and shields hit was nearly deafening.

Cara ran like never before, her sword hitting and crashing with the other creature's shields and swords as she searched the army for Sarith. She dipped and dove through the fights and made her way near the back of them all, closer to the bridge at the far end of the lake. Creature after creature went down, the smell of blood filling the air. She jumped over the few casualties in her way, but she scarcely noticed. She ran up onto the bridge and there she saw her; Sarith was closing in fast. Cara fought the few creatures that came towards her, but as Sarith approached, they moved like waves out of her way. They knew Sarith was the one that was to finish Cara herself.

Sarith stopped only a few feet away from Cara and held her sword up high as war raged on around them.

"You really think you are a match for me?" Sarith remarked, smirking at her. "You have NO idea what I'm capable of!" She swung her sword around in front of her, laughing as she looked Cara up and down.

"This land is mine and always will be. Darkness always wins in the end." Sarith held her sword up, ready to fight.

Darkness may have won so many battles in her life before, but not today, Cara thought as she faced Sarith.

Cara held up her sword with one hand and put her other hand out. From Cara's free hand, a fireball formed and she held it for a moment, before throwing it towards Sarith, dropping it only a foot in front of her.

"Oh, look at that!" Sarith grinned. "I had heard you had magic, but I had truly doubted it." She threw her sword down to the ground and put her hands close together and sparks flew. A ball formed in her hands and it grew, twice as large as Cara's, and she sent it flying towards her.

Cara swung her shield around from her back and it hit, sending her flying back several feet towards the bridge. Cara cringed, but scrambled to her feet. She threw down her sword too and put her hands out in front of her. She could feel the heat rising in her hands and she shot flames towards Sarith. Sarith saw it coming and raised her arms up. The water in the pond twisted into a funnel and quickly shot up, forming a wall that quickly extinguished them, steam sizzling and rising in the air.

They both stopped for a moment and eyed each other. They were equally surprised at the other's ability. Then Sarith charged. She hit Cara hard in the gut, sending her onto her back, now with Sarith on top, her hands groping for Cara's throat. Cara struggled and fought, but Sarith's grip found her throat and she started squeezing.

Cara couldn't breathe. She hit Sarith and struggled, but it was like Sarith had super strength. Her vision filled with spots and darkness crept into her field of vision. Cara was terrified. She couldn't die like this.

She scratched at the arms that held her, trying to peel the fingertips from her skin, but the strength in her own arms was failing her. The darkness in her vision only got worse. Her hands dropped to her sides. She was losing. This would be the end. Everyone had been right all along.

Then Sarith was gone. Cara gasped for breath, coughing hard. She turned and saw that Sarith was lying on her back a few feet away on the bridge, winded. Behind Cara stood Woodrow, shield in hand. He had knocked Sarith off. Cara struggled to her feet, rubbing her neck and waiting for her head to clear. He tossed Cara his sword and nodded. Cara caught it and turned to Sarith. She was already sitting back up. Cara took a deep breath and charged.

Sarith scrambled to her feet and just as Cara was about to hit, she ducked down. Cara's legs collided with her body and sent Cara flying toward the path. She slammed into the ground, and her nose broke. Blood gushed out. Cara gingerly touched it and looked at the blood on her fingers. Sarith watched her and laughed.

"See? I told you I was stronger. What a silly little girl, thinking that she's anything more than just ordinary," Sarith hissed at her.

"Not anymore!" Cara said, taking a deep breath.

Cara charged so fast, Sarith didn't see it coming. They hit and Sarith lost her footing. Together they flipped over the handrail of the bridge and plunged into the icy lake water, everything going instantly quiet. They surfaced and Cara swam over to her and wrapped her hands around Sarith's throat. Sarith grabbed at the hands that were growing tighter and tighter, trying to pry them off. They dipped in and out of the water, thrashing as they struggled against each other. Cara watched as clouds of unconsciousness clouded Sarith's vision. She had her now. This would be the end. All Cara had to do was hold on and all this darkness would end. There would be no more night-mares, no more fear or terror from the beast. She knew it was almost done. She looked into Sarith's eyes again, and saw them fall, her face going deep crimson red. The life was almost gone.

Suddenly, Cara's hand released and she looked at them, not even recognizing them anymore. She wasn't a killer. She might get mad and hate when she was bullied, teased, and taunted, but even despite that, this wasn't her. Sarith coughed and slowly caught her breath. She looked over at Cara and grabbed Cara roughly by the shoulders and pushed her down deep into the water. Sarith flipped around until she was on top of Cara, pushing her down into the water further and further. Cara's eyes bulged and she struggled. Her head flipped back and forth as she looked around her, seeing only the mud and rocks under the bridge. She fought against Sarith, but her strength was failing her. Cara looked down at the bottom of the lake and saw the light coming from beyond. It was softer than she expected and she thought it was going to be bigger, but there it was, just barely shining through the floating dirt.

As Sarith pushed them down further and further to-wards it, Cara finally realized it wasn't the light at the end of her life. It was the tunnel. After all this time, it was still there. Cara felt a fresh wave of adrenaline rush through her. She spun and pushed Sarith away, putting distance between them. She made her way to the surface and took a deep breath. Sarith came up beside her but this time Cara grabbed her. Cara kicked against the water as hard as she could, and pulled Sarith down with her. She dragged her down towards the tunnel. Sarith tried to struggle, but even she was getting tired. They entered and the light faded to black, but she knew that there was only one way to go. Sarith had lost the strength to fight and let herself be pulled along.

Sarith quickly turned to deadweight and when Cara felt like she couldn't go any further, she saw the light coming from overhead. The end of the tunnel was near. Cara kicked again and again, focusing on that patch of light.

Her lungs ached for breath and just as she wanted to give up, she finally broke through the surface of the water and she gasped. Her lungs burned as fresh oxygen filled her again. They had made it back to the school. Her legs ached from kicking, but she pushed on, pulling the now dead weight of Sarith with her towards the shallow end of the pool where the stairs were. She pulled her body up as high as she could muster up the steps and stopped. She flipped Sarith onto her back and although her arms barely cooperated; she began shaky chest compressions and blowing air into her lungs. With every compression and every breath, Cara felt like she would collapse, but she couldn't let this woman die.

And just as Cara thought she couldn't do anymore, Sarith coughed and turned to her side, spitting water out of her lungs and mouth.

Cara fell back onto the stairs and laid there, unable to move, her whole body aching. Her breathing was so ragged she didn't think she'd ever catch it again.

They stayed that way for several minutes before Sarith sat up and looked down at Cara.

"You. This is not over!" Sarith whispered as she moved her hands close together, waiting for her magic to form another ball of sparks, but nothing happened. She tried over and over, but still nothing.

Cara stayed where she was, willing her body to move.

A whisper came across her lips and hit Sarith hard.

"No magic here. Welcome back to the real world."

Thirty-Nine

When her strength finally came back, Cara got to her feet and headed towards the door. Sarith slowly trudged behind her.

"Where are you going?" Sarith asked as they neared the door.

"Home. You can't do anything to me here. And I want to go see my family." She pushed open the door and took a step, but quickly noticed Sarith wasn't following. She just stood there.

"Don't you have a home that you can go to? They said you came from this world a long time ago, so there must be somewhere to go."

Sarith paused for a moment, those words echoing through her head. Slowly, Cara saw the look in Sarith's eyes change. Memories of things past were finally coming back to her.

"A little girl," she murmured, as the memories were being pulled from a distant place in her mind.

"She had flowing, blonde hair and her eyes... They were like sparkling emerald stones. They were just like someone else. Oh my, my husband!" Cara watched as Sarith backed up and had tears well up in her eyes. "How did I forget about him? It's been so long. What if they don't want me back?"

"You won't know if you don't at least try," Cara said. "Go find them. I'm sure they will be happy to see you."

"Melissa," she said, her eyes coming back into focus and looked at Cara. "I don't even know how old she would be at this point. Cara, I'm... I'm sorry. To you and to the others. I let myself be overtaken by the love of power."

"Did you just say Melissa?"

"I have to find her." Sarith walked over to the far wall and looked at the calendar.

"Is that date right?" Sarith asked, pointing to the year.

"Yes, it is."

"How is this possible? I was there for... years. Melissa would be about seventeen now. I might not even recognize her anymore."

"Do you know what school we're in?" Cara asked.

"Yes, I remember this. She would go to this school if they still live in the area."

Cara could feel her guard coming up again. Melissa was her daughter. That explained so much. Melissa was a bully because her mom was gone. She was upset and looking for acceptance.

"I know who your daughter is." She hesitated slightly, but made herself stop. Sarith wasn't the same person she was before all this happened. "If you go to the school office, they will get her for you."

Sarith looked down at her soaking wet outfit and fidgeted with it slightly before finally letting her eyes meet Cara's.

"What if she doesn't want to see me again?" Sarith said, suddenly looking so much smaller than she had before.

"Why wouldn't she? You're her mother."

"We had this horrible fight right before I left. I... I didn't mean to leave, it just sort of happened," Sarith said, her hands falling to her sides.

"Just talk to her. You don't know until you try."

Sarith nodded, lost in thought for a moment, before looking up again at Cara.

"I know this is probably too little, too late, but thank you for bringing me back." It came out so awkwardly but Cara knew her heart was genuine.

"I should probably go," Sarith said. "And I'm sorry for everything. Life hasn't been kind to me here. It's really taken a toll on me. But I'm going to try and change."

"I know what that's like," said Cara. "I've dealt with my fair share of things too."

Sarith took a deep breath and pointed to the doorway before walking past Cara and to it. She took one last look at Cara and smiled, before pushing it open and disappearing down the hall.

* * *

"Where have you been?" Her parents, Mike and Stephanie, embraced her, squeezing almost too tightly as she entered their home. The small bungalow had always seemed so cozy before, but now, with the officer inside, it felt so small. Her mom cried and hugged her, then cried some more. Her dad had been busy talking to the officer.

Cara looked over their shoulders at the cop nearby, unsure what to tell them.

"I've been..." Her voice trailed off and she didn't know where to begin. How would she tell them where she had been and what all she had seen?

They let her go and Stephanie slouched down to look into her eyes, searching for any kind of answer.

"What happened to your nose?" her mother exclaimed, looking over the rest of her for scraps and bruises.

"Oh, it's okay. It barely hurts," Cara lied, not wanting them to worry more than they had already.

They escorted her into the living room and sat on the couch. Mike brought over a sweaty glass of water and Cara happily took it. Across the room, the officer who had been watching her intently had his pen poised above a well-worn notepad in hand.

"What can you tell us about where you've been?" he asked, ready to write.

She took a sip, pondering what to say. How much detail could she give before they thought she was making it all up?

So, Cara began slowly and chose her words carefully. She didn't want anyone to get the wrong idea about any of this, so she told them all about the Hammer chasing her.

The cop asked her about the bruises but she quickly said she didn't want to press charges. She told them about how she ended up in the pool, swimming deeper and deeper, but then she stopped. She couldn't tell them about the other world. They would think she was insane. And where would that land her? Would they want to have her see a therapist? And would her parents really believe that she could defeat someone as strong as Sarith? She had always been a quiet, meek person. She had never had the guts to do anything like this before. And yet, somehow, she had.

She looked from the cop to her parents and back. It would be better for everyone if they didn't know.

"I got to the bottom of the pool, and uh, I really don't remember what happened after that. The next thing I remember was waking up in the school and knowing that I needed to come home."

The officer stopped writing and nodded. He wrote something, then tucked his notebook into this pocket, but not before Cara saw the word "runaway" written in big letters and underlined.

"Well, I am glad you're home. That's what matters most to me!" Her mom hugged her again, then went over to the cop to talk to him, motioning that he should join her in the other room so Cara wouldn't hear.

Mike looked at her daughter for a long time before turning to the refrigerator.

"Well, kiddo, I'm glad you're okay. I was worried," he said, head buried in the fridge.

"I know. I'm sorry."

"Nothing to be sorry about," he said, pulling a bottle of juice out of the fridge and letting the door close behind him. "Funny how the memory works, though, isn't it? I've found that sometimes it takes a while before I finally re-member. Other times? It's like the memory never even left me."

She saw the look in his eyes. He knew there was more that she remembered, but how much, she wasn't sure. It would be easier to tell someone, even if he thought she was crazy, but was it worth it?

She looked at him and opened her mouth to talk, but the cop and her mom walked in.

"I'm going to go for now, but if you remember anything, anything at all, I want you to call me. If this matter needs to take this matter further, then I'll do so."

The police officer handed her a business card with the station's number and, in his handwriting, his cellphone number. She tucked it in her pocket and watched as he walked out the front door.

"I know I just got back, but would you be okay if I went to my room for a bit and just... rested?" Cara asked.

"Sure dear," Stephanie said, exchanging a concerned look with dad but quickly tried to hide it, "we'll be nearby if you need us."

She ran over to Cara one final time and gave her a hug so tight it nearly knocked the wind out of her.

"I'm sorry, mom. If I can share anything more, I will." Cara said. Stephanie reached over and cupped her face in her hands. Cara looked into her mom's grey eyes and saw nothing but love. It made her want to tell her more, but not just yet.

Cara headed upstairs to her room and paused at the doorway. The room looked different. The posters on the walls of her favourite bands were still there, along with the piles of fantasy books beside the bed. There were a few of her childhood stuffed animals on the bed, along with her bright pink journal. It looked like the room of someone so much younger than her. She couldn't believe that it was the same place.

Closing the door behind her, she threw the things off her bed and let herself collapse on it. It was so soft and inviting. She had missed this bed. Her mind slowly drifted to all she had been through and the animals that she already missed dearly. She wished she could have gotten to say a proper goodbye. Woodrow and Cynthia had been so good to her. And James for saving her life that first day, then finding her a place to stay safe while she was there. He never gave up on her, even when she didn't believe in herself. He always knew somehow that she would defeat Sarith.

Swirls of sleep came in and as her thoughts drifted, sleep overtook her and she felt herself falling. It was slow at first, but without warning, it came on quick and she was lost into a dreamless sleep.

Forty

A few days later, when her nose and other injuries were mostly healed, Cara convinced her mother to let her return to school. Sitting at home, under the watchful eyes of her parents, was driving her nuts. She could barely pee by herself because they were so worried about her. But each day, they gave her another inch of freedom and she could see they were trying.

As she left that morning, she walked out of the house and straightened her shoulders back and held her head up high. She didn't know what would come her way when she finally walked in that front door of the school, but she was ready to take it on. The look of shock and confusion on Sarith's face that day when she understood Cara was stronger than she had expected gave her so much confidence. It was the last time she would ever let someone think less of her. She was interested to see how Melissa and her cronies would react to this new, confident person.

As she walked down the hall of the school, what had once felt like a monstrous place suddenly felt so small.

Ahead of her, she could see Melissa, leaning against a row of lockers, talking with her group. Normally, she would have stopped and tried to go another way to avoid them, but not today.

As she passed Melissa, the girl turned and looked at her; her face full of disgust.

"Look who finally came back to school," Melissa said as she pushed off the locker and moved to stand in front of her, blocking the way. "What? Did you forget what I said about coming near me, you freak?"

Cara stopped and looked her dead in the eye. Suddenly, she didn't look as scary as she used to either. Eye-to-eye with her, she wasn't smaller than Melissa like she always thought.

"I can walk where I want," Cara said, not letting her eye contact falter from Melissa.

Melissa stammered slightly, not expecting that. They stood frozen for a moment, surprised at Cara's confidence. Cara had never talked to her or her groupies like that before, and it felt good. Melissa shook her head and quickly got her bearings back.

"That's what you think," she said finally and lifted her head to the girl beside her.

The impact of the Hammer's fist into Cara's stomach stunned her. She hadn't seen her. Cara fell to the floor, grasping for breath. Melissa's laughter ringing in her ears. Her blood boiled. She staggered to her feet and looked at Melissa. All around her, other students stood still, unsure what to do. Cara paused for only a moment before lunging on Melissa and threw punch after punch, her hands instantly burning as her skin and bones made contact. Then something cracked inside her and Cara howled in pain. She looked up and saw the Hammer above her, holding a textbook that looked too big to be real. She had hit Cara in the shoulder, sending pains throughout her.

The Hammer grabbed her arm and pulled hard, sending fireworks into Cara's vision. She was spun around and pushed down towards the ground again while Melissa scurried away. Melissa paused only for a moment, smiling at Cara through blood-stained teeth before shouting to the Hammer to do it.

The girls then stomped so hard on Cara's shoulder that a loud pop echoed in her ears.

A ear-piercing scream came to her ears. She didn't know it was her own until suddenly it was cut off and the world went black.

Forty-One

"Cara! Come back to us. Cara!" She heard a voice drifting through the darkness and the void she was floating in. Her eyes fluttered open, and for a moment, she looked around, her eyes wild with fear.

"It's okay. Vanessa has been taken care of," the nurse said, standing beside the bed, watching the numbers on the screen bounce around while she recorded them.

"What?" Cara mumbled through swollen-feeling lips. She reached up with her good arm and felt her face. There were bandages on her forehead and chin, and her upper lip was fat and puffy.

"The girl that did this to you."

Cara didn't understand. What was this woman talking about? Cara tried to sit up and her world spun. Every part of her hurt.

"Don't get up," the nurse said, gently nudging her back down. "You are at the hospital. You got into a fight with Melissa and her friend Vanessa."

"Vanessa?"

"She's the one that dislocated your shoulder."

"Oh," Cara murmured. She had never heard her actual name before.

Cara took a deep breath and winced as her body screamed out in pain. Everything seemed to hurt, but her shoulder was by far the worse. She tried to shift herself to a better sitting position, but was struggling. The nurse helped her move and tilted the bed a bit more so she could see better.

Cara's eyes scanned what she could see of the room and finally noticed the beeping in the corner. Tubs ran into her nose and arm, while machines blinked, beeped, and hummed. An armchair that sat beside the bed had her mom's sweater thrown over it.

"Your mom's getting coffee," the nurse said, noticing the direction Cara's eyes had taken. "We didn't think you'd wake up this soon. It was a pretty nasty fight you guys got into. You're cut up and bruised, not to mention the dislocated shoulder. We're waiting on some test results to let us know if there's any internal bleeding, but we don't think you have any. It's more of a precaution. Are you able to tell me what happened?"

Cara gently shook her head. She knew exactly what happened, but it wouldn't matter if she told them or not. Melissa and her friends would always win. That's the way it always was.

"You're awake!" Her mom said, entering the room and nearly dropping the coffee cups in her hands.

"Yeah, I'm okay," Cara mumbled.

"What in the world happened?" Stephanie pulled the chair up beside the bed. It scraped along the floor loudly, making Cara winced.

The nurse gave her good arm a light squeeze and gave her a knowing look.

"When you're ready," she whispered before she turned and walked out the door, closing it quietly behind her.

"How do you feel?" her mom asked, then stopped and shook her head. "Stupid question. Sorry. I got myself a coffee, but I got you juice. I figured it would be easier to drink something with a straw right now, seeing as your lip is swollen. Now I'm wondering if I should have gotten myself one instead of a coffee." She took a deep breath and looked at Cara.

Cara could read her mom's face like a painting. She always had. The worry lines had only gotten deeper over the years. And today they almost were overwhelming to look at.

"I'm okay." Cara readjusted, wincing at the pain that now shot up her body again.

"You're far from okay!" her mom said, standing to look down at her daughter. "Was it her again?"

"What?"

"You know what I'm talking about: Melissa and her thugs. The Hammer, as you call her."

Cara stopped and looked at her mom, wondering how she knew. She never talked about. She didn't even journal about it. And honestly, Cara didn't want anyone to know and try to fix it, because she knew it would only make things worse. She had always figured she'd be able to handle it on her own and she had tried, but she never thought they would be this hard to stop.

Her mom handed her the juice and took a sip of her steaming cup of coffee. Cara took a drink, not sure what to say.

"How?"

"Your music teacher said something at the parent-teacher interviews last week, while you were in the bathroom," her mom replied. "But I had my suspicions that something was happening. You haven't been yourself for months. I figured either you really hated school or something more was going on."

Cara looked out the window beside her bed and sighed. It looked like a perfect day. Her mind slowly wandered to Woodrow and Cynthia. She hoped they were having more fun than she was.

"I wish you would have told me. I can't do anything unless you say something," Stephanie said.

"I know." Cara took another sip and carefully put the cup down on the tray in front of her. "I wanted to take care of it myself. I thought I could, especially after…" Cara stopped herself.

"After what? Do you remember something about where you've been?" Stephanie put her hand on Cara's.

Cara wanted to tell her. Everything in her said she should, but the words stumbled in her mouth and they just wouldn't come out. Her mom saw the hesitation and turned away. She distracted herself with something in her purse.

"When you're ready," she said. "Maybe for now, you should get some sleep."

Cara didn't know how she'd managed to sleep with all the beeping of machines around her, but as she lay there, the deep envelope of darkness came over her. She felt herself slip and fall backwards into the world of dreams.

* * *

Cara opened her eyes and found herself back at the lake, only now it was a thick, deep hole of wet, sticky mud. She gasped and looked down at it from the bridge. Water slowly oozed out of the clay and the little bit of water there was still moving. She blinked. She was now standing in it, her feet trapped.

What the —, she thought, as she attempted to pull her foot free. This liquid held fast, causing Cara to sway uneasily. She pulled hard, and it released, but her shoe was lost. She was reaching, grabbing, hoping to get out, but this unforgiving substance wouldn't allow it. Instead, it was slowly eating her body; consuming her in its warm grasp.

Gradually, it devoured her shins and thighs before inching its way to her stomach. She looked for anything nearby that would help her escape, but the only thing close was a weed. She reached for it, even though she knew it wouldn't help her at all, but as she moved, she felt herself sinking a little more. It held too firmly. It continued its dance upwards towards her chest. Already it was getting harder and harder to breathe.

Cara's eyes whipped back and forth across the shoreline, looking for anyone to save her. Then out of the bushes right in front of her was Melissa, with Vanessa the Hammer, and the other two girls that Cara still hadn't learnt their names. They all stood there, arms crossed, greedy smiles on their faces.

"Help! Please!" Cara cried out to them, but it was met with laughter. She could feel herself slipping further and further, and panic gripped her.

Behind them, the trees shook and the ground vibrated. She let her eyes move up ever so slowly as it got louder and more intense. Then, the beast emerged, towering over them before he sat, his behind hitting the ground, causing the girls to jump slightly, but they held their ground.

The beast let his tongue slip out and he panted slightly. He cocked his head to the side and grinned, showing his mincing teeth. Cara knew he was enjoying seeing this happening to her.

The thick mud continued to creep up her neck to her chin, her breaths coming ragged with fear. She shook, waiting for the moment when this mud-like substance would enter her. After an eternity of waiting, it entered her mouth. She could taste the mixture of water and earth. It was thick and almost choking. In the next moment, it tangoed up to her nose. Shaking violently, she felt it waltz first into her left nostril, then her right, cutting off her air supply. She tried to move her head so her nose would at least be out of it, but it held her like nothing before. She looked at the girls and the beast, just sitting there in amusement, waiting for that ultimate moment.

She closed her eyes in resignation and it finished eating. This warm, mud-like substance was like a moist, tight hug that wouldn't let her go. And just as her body began screaming for fresh oxygen, her lungs aching for a fresh breath, she jolted awake; her hair and pillow soaked with sweat. Thoughts raced through her as she tried to clear the image that now felt ingrained in her mind. It had felt so real.

"Honey, are you okay? You look white as a ghost. Your pulse is absolutely racing." The nurse turned and watched the numbers and bars dancing across the screen. Cara tried to catch her breath, but it came in shallow amounts.

"You must have been having a nightmare. Take a deep breath. It's okay now. It was only a bad dream."

Cara sat up and looked at her. Bad dream? But there shouldn't be bad dreams anymore, not after bringing Sarith here. Sarith only had powers in that magical world, and with no magic here, there shouldn't be any chance of it. Something was wrong. She must have missed something. And if she did, that could mean that her friends were in danger. She had to get back. She had to see if they were okay.

"My mom?" she asked the nurse, not seeing her around.

"Oh, it's after visiting hours. She went home, but she said she'd be back first thing in the morning."

Cara laid back on the bed and closed her eyes. Beyond her quick breaths, she made out the sound of the monitor and she forced herself to focus on it. She tried to match the methodical beeps to her breathing. She could feel her heartbeat slow and she was finally calm again.

Repositioning herself to sit, she watched the nurse doing her duties.

"How does everything look?" she asked. She leaned to the right to try and look at the monitors herself. She watched as the nurse took the long receipt paper of her vitals in her hands and looked it over.

"This is looking much better. Your pulse is calming." She stepped towards Cara and tripped on the cord to the monitor. She put her hands out and caught herself on the edge of the bed. The system erupted with alarms and flashing lights.

"Sorry. I can be so clumsy sometimes!" The nurse said, righting herself and heading back to the monitors. She plugged it back in, tucking the loose cords under the bed and then pushed a few buttons. Cara watched, remembering the sequence.

"Are you okay?" Cara asked.

"Oh, yeah. I just need to pay better attention. These silly cables," the nurse said.

"Any idea if I will have to stay here much longer?" Cara asked.

"Well, the doctor should be in shortly, but I have a feeling you'll be just fine," she winked as she came over to Cara. The nurse checked the IV in her arm and the electrodes on her chest to be sure everything was secure.

"I think you'll be on your way home in no time. For now, just be sure to rest. You've been through a lot."

Cara returned her smile and thanked her as the nurse slipped out of the room.

Cara sat up and leaned forward to make sure no one was coming near the doorway. Satisfied, she looked at the monitors. She was pretty sure she knew what she had to do to quiet the alarms once the electrodes were off her chest. But could she really run out on her family right now? She had just gotten back. Only the sick feeling in her stomach only got worse. There had to be something going on that she didn't know about in that other world. Why else would she have had such a horrible nightmare? Maybe she should leave a note. That way, she could at least let them know she wouldn't be gone long.

She looked around and saw her shoes on the floor over by the door, and her socks balled up inside. Her coat was on the back of the chair her mom had been in earlier. If she was quick, she could probably be out the door before anyone even noticed.

Suddenly the doctor appeared in the window, looking down at her chart. Cara jumped back into bed. The door opened and Cara threw the covers over herself.

He walked in, head down, studying the thin brown file folder in his hands. He took a moment before finally looking up at her.

"Hello, Cara. I'm Dr. Robbins. We got the test results back from the tests we ran earlier and everything seems in order. There is no internal bleeding, which is very good. The shoulder was dislocated but it should be fine. You will have to wear a sling for a bit until it has a chance to heal some. The nose wasn't broken, but it is deeply bruised, so it will take some time to heal. It will probably be painful for a while. But otherwise, everything else is surface, so it should heal in a few weeks. You will need to be careful and not get into any more fights, though."

The doctor paused. She didn't know what he expected, but she wasn't about to say anything. He could think what he wanted.

After a moment, he cleared his throat and closed the folder.

"We're going to keep you overnight so we can monitor everything. The nurse is going to come in shortly and change your bandages, too. Be sure to get some rest. That will help you the most right now. But as long as nothing changes, you'll head home tomorrow."

Cara laid back, happy to hear that she was mostly alright. He checked the monitor one last time before slipping out the door and leaving her on her own.

Instantly, she grabbed a pad of paper and pen by the phone and scribbled a quick note to her parents. She didn't want them to worry, but she also couldn't tell them the truth. She just wrote: "Had something important I had to do. I will be back tomorrow. Everything's fine. I'm okay. Don't worry about me. I love you all." Leaving it by the phone, she carefully got up. In the hall, there were people milling around, but everyone seemed so distracted she didn't think anyone would notice. She tiptoed over to the monitor and found the buttons the nurse had used before to restart the machine. As it powered down, she pulled the IV free and tossed it into the bowl the nurse had brought her dessert in. She ripped the electrodes off her chest and let them fall down the side of the machine. Ducking down, she slid over to her shoes and carefully pulled them on.

Under the chair she found an overnight bag that her mom must have forgotten to tell her about. Inside was a change of clothes and some toiletries.

Cara threw the hospital gown onto the floor, changed, then grabbed her jacket. She carefully put it on, and stood. She felt a bit wobbly, but she knew if she was careful, she'd be okay. One final glance out the window, she saw the hallway was much quieter. Carefully, she pulled the door open and poked her head out. Cara slipped out of her room and walked up the hall. She didn't know this hospital well yet, but she followed the signs leading out to the street. She turned down the hall and banged into a bed set up along one of the walls. Pain shot up her bad arm and she squealed.

"Miss?" she heard someone call from behind her, but she didn't stop. She darted around the bed and pushed on. "Miss?"

It sounded like the nurse she had seen earlier in her room but she didn't dare turn back to see.

"I think that's the girl that came in with the shoulder," she heard the nurse say to someone behind her. Cara quickened her pace and turned left, then right, trying to find her way. She heard footsteps coming towards her fast. She turned again and saw the doors to the outside.

"Stop her!" she heard the nurse shout at someone.

Cara was almost there. She ran. She hit the doors roughly with her good arm and pushed with everything in her. It gave way and the cool night air hit, instantly energizing her. The sidewalk wasn't busy, but the cafe across the street was. She ran as fast as her mangled body would allow, and she yanked the door open and darted inside. She turned and ducked behind someone sitting at a table, laptop in front of them. They turned and looked at her funny, as she squatted down beside them, but she pretended to tie her shoelace.

Through the legs under the tables, she saw the nurse, along with a security guard and an orderly looking around the street for her, but they hadn't seen her. She waited, switching feet to fake tie her other shoe. The guy looked at her again, but noticed her doing the other shoe and shrugged.

When she finally saw them head back inside, she slowly stood and turned to the counter.

"Water please?" she asked and took a deep breath. She'd give herself a few more minutes to gather her thoughts, then she was going back.

Forty-Two

The clock above the cafe's counter read eight o'clock. It had been a half hour since she had seen the nurse and the security guard go back inside.

She left the cafe and walked towards the school down the street. Cara had to get back to her friends and find out what was going on.

She knew the back door of the school would be open for another half hour. The local band practiced there twice a week. As she pushed the door open, she could hear them in a nearby room. The music sounded fine, but she knew the trumpet section was about half a beat behind.

Peeking around the corner of the hall, she found it empty. She walked as confidently as she could muster down it and towards the pool, and opened the door.

Inside, she heard voices and found Melissa and her groupies talking.

"You feel bad? Are you kidding me? She's a freak and she doesn't deserve to breathe."

"I'm just saying, maybe we went too far this time. I've been suspended from school and my dad is threatening military school. My mom just came back. I can't be sent away right now," Melissa said.

"Your mom left you for years! She didn't call, write, nothing. And you're planning to forgive her just like that?" the Hammer said.

"You don't know the whole story," Melissa said.

"I don't need to. I know she left when you needed her and that's why we're here," the Hammer said.

Melissa said something back to her, but she said it in such a low tone Cara couldn't hear it. Cara was about to take a step in, then she heard a splash.

She poked her head around the door and saw the Hammer standing over the edge of the pool, watching the rippling surface. Her eyes were roaring with fire and revenge.

Melissa's head came up from the water and gasped.

"What are you doing?" Melissa asked, trying to get over to the edge.

The Hammer crouched down to grab her.

"Hey!" Melissa shouted, trying to get away.

Cara immediately felt like she had time travelled. This girl had done the same thing to her. Would Melissa survive a watery attack? Cara ran across to the pool and jumped in. Everyone turned.

"Take a deep breath!" She said into Melissa's ear when she reached her.

They both took deep breaths before diving deep into the water. Cara pointed to the bottom of the pool and Melissa followed her. They made their way to the tunnel below. Cara's dislocated shoulder made swimming nearly impossible. She kicked as best she could but it was slow going for her. She struggled to get herself through. Melissa turned and hooked her arm around her and helped pull her through the water and finally to the lake on the other side.

They surfaced and slowly made their way to the shoreline. They both collapsed on the sand and tried to catch their breath. Cara rolled herself onto her side and looked around.

Sarith and her had arrived there to battle only yesterday, but it felt like a lifetime ago; almost like a weird dream. There was no sign of the battle anywhere, not even footprints in the sand. In fact, there was no sign of anyone around. Everything was so quiet when normally it was teaming with life.

"Where did you bring me?" Melissa finally asked as she sat up. She shielded her eyes from the sun and took in the view before finally letting her eyes settle on Cara.

"It's a long story. I'll tell you on the way," Cara said, finally sitting.

Melissa stood and turned to Cara, extending a hand down to her to help her up. Cara looked at it, unsure of this kind gesture but took it. They walked away from the water and towards the forest. Cara had a lot to tell her and they didn't have much time.

Forty-Three

Cara started at the beginning. She told her about the day that she was chased into the pool, how she went through the tunnel like they just had and how there was something terrorizing the world here. She told her about the type-writers and how the dreams worked. Melissa shook her head so many times it made Cara's own head spin.

"This is ridiculous. You know that, right? Is this some weird sort of payback for everything?"

"You can't be serious," Cara said, trudging through the forest. "Do you see where we are? Why would I lie about something like this? Or make it up, or whatever it is you think I did."

"It wouldn't surprise me if you made this up! You're such a, a—"

"Enough!" Cara spun around and Melissa stopped just short of colliding with her.

"What?"

"Enough! Listen, I get it. You hate me. I don't know why, but for some reason you do. But you know what? It doesn't matter. I don't care if you like or hate me. But from what I could see in the school there, was that your 'friends,'" she said, making air quotes when she said it, "looked like they were about to pound you into salt, just like they did with me." Cara carefully raised her right arm, showing the hurt shoulder.

"And I wasn't about to let someone else get hurt by them because frankly, it hurts like hell and I will not stand by and do nothing."

A crow cawed overhead and Melissa looked up for a moment at the canopy of trees. She dug her toe into the soil below and finally met Cara's eyes.

"We got into a lot of trouble doing that to you," Melissa finally said as she sat on a nearby boulder.

"Yeah, I bet." Cara sat on a nearby tree stump and rubbed her bad arm, hoping to relieve some of the pain.

"They were threatening to expel us, which normally I wouldn't have cared about. But this time, my dad is threatening military school. He figures it'll do me some good." Melissa reached up and rubbed her forehead. She cleared her throat before speaking again.

"Only, my mom just got back." Her words saturated with emotion. Cara waited as she coughed and cleared her throat.

"She had been gone for years. She was trying to explain where she has been and trying to get us to be a family again and I think I want that. My dad has been struggling with the idea but I think he's finally getting on board. And if I go away, I won't be around her again! I can't do that. Vanessa was the one fighting me on it. She doesn't care.

She's been expelled for what she did. Her parents are actually sending her to military school."

"Your mom just got back?" Cara said, not sure how to tell her what she knew.

"Yeah, everything she's told me sounds ridiculous, like some kind of dream: all about animals and dreams. I don't know. All I know is that..." Her voice trailed off and she looked down at her feet again. Cara was taken aback by this. Normally, Melissa had such a confident and strong way about her, but today, she wasn't.

"You're glad she's back," Cara said, sitting down on a boulder.

"Yeah, I am, but at the same time, I don't know," Melissa said, joining her.

"What makes you say that?" Cara asked.

"Before she left, we got into this big fight. I drove her away. She says that I didn't, but I know that's why she left. I said some horrible things."

"I'm sure she'll forgive you. A lot has happened since then," Cara said.

"I guess so, but what if I say something like that again and drive her away?" Melissa asked.

"Trust me, Sarith isn't going anywhere. I could tell she was happy to be back when she thought of you."

Melissa's eyes darted up to Cara, stunned.

"How do you know her name?"

"I was the one that brought her back," Cara said, rubbing away the uncomfortable feeling that was making its way up her neck.

"What?"

"That's the part I hadn't told you yet," Cara said, leaning back. She then told her Sarith's part in this world and how Cara had to stop her.

"She was the one that I had to defeat to make these animals safe. I had to get her out of their lives. I didn't harm her, it's not who I am, but I managed to get her back through the tunnel and back to the real world."

"You?" Melissa asked, stunned.

"Yes. But can I tell you something? I don't think she meant to go away from as long as she did. This place, it almost does something to your memories. I know I felt it when I was here before. When we both came back, before we left the school, we talked. I told her she needs to make things right. And with everything she went through and thinking she had lost you, I think she wants to let the past go.

"Maybe you don't have to let her in totally right now, but maybe you could give her a chance. Even if it's from a distance. Let her take you to coffee. Let her talk to you about what she's done here, even if it sounds completely nuts. I could tell she loves you and wants to make things right," Cara said.

Melissa finally met Cara's eyes.

"You see that? In her?" Melissa said.

"I think so. I see it in you, too."

Melissa flung her arms around Cara and squeezed.

Cara flinched from the pain and Melissa quickly let go.

"Sorry, I'm still tender," Cara said, rubbing her shoulder.

"Cara, I'm so sorry for everything we've done to you. I don't know if you'll ever forgive me, but I hope you'll give me a chance," Melissa said, eyeing Cara's shoulder.

"What about your groupies?" Cara said, shifting her spot.

"I'll make sure they stay away. Plus, Vanessa was expelled. Either way, I'm ready for some new friends, anyway. Know anyone that could use one?" Melissa asked.

Cara lightly shoved her.

"I forgive you. And hopefully you'll consider giving your mom a chance too," Cara said, standing up and stretching.

"I will. So, now that we've got that figured out, where are we going?" Melissa asked, also standing.

"We're going to town. I have to find my friends. Once I took your mom back to the real world, I still ended up having a nightmare, which means something's wrong. I had removed the only bad person from this world, yet the nightmares continued. I need to find out what's going on."

The two of them raced through the forest and came up to the town and halted.

It was in ruins. Cara ran through the rubble-filled streets towards Woodrow's home. She could feel herself panicking.

"Woodrow! Woodrow!" Cara called as she came up to what was left of his once cozy home. The surrounding gardens were now ash and charred remains. The home itself was gone and the only thing still standing was the chimney. She could still picture them sitting in front of it, a throw blanket on her legs and the two of them watching the flames dance.

She looked at Melissa and all around her but no one was to be seen. The area had been completely abandoned. Her mind went to the worst possibility that no one was left. Waves of nausea came over her and she bent over, trying to keep her lunch down.

Then the ground rumbled. She turned and far in the distance, she could see the beast coming at them. Melissa screamed. He was three times the size he had been before. Now, he could step on three small homes with a single step. He ran full speed, blocking out the afternoon sun and making a getaway seemed impossible.

Cara screamed and stumbled over the rumble, trying to find somewhere to hide. He was closing in and every step was like an earthquake. Cara was shaking so badly from his impact and her own fear that she felt as though she was getting nowhere at all. He was thirty feet away now, closing in fast. Her breathing was ragged.

Twenty feet. She could feel his hot, sour breath coming at her like a wave.

Ten feet. She stumbled. Stars flashed in her eyes. She tried to catch her balance and raised both arms quickly in the air. Her shoulder. She withered in pain. Melissa ran over and tried to help her, but it was too late.

This was it. Cara threw her good arm up over her head and braced for it. The breath was now so hot it brought tears to her eyes.

A hand reached over and grabbed her ankle, and yanked it down. She felt herself falling, far and away from the beast and into a void. Cara slammed into the cold ground and yelped. She grabbed her shoulder and cried. Tears flowed freely. Through the vale of tears, she saw Melissa sit up quickly beside her and scream. Cara turned. Before her was a lion. She wiped away the tears and as Melissa tried to crawl backwards away from it, Cara laughed.

"You came!" came a voice she recognized immediately. Terrance scanned her up and down, not believing his eyes. She stood and threw her good arm around him, only a little more dishevelled.

"It's okay. He's a friend of mine," Cara said, releasing Terrance and helping Melissa to her feet. She kept her distance but Cara grabbed the lion's enormous paw and held it. Even in the low light of the tunnels, he looked just as great as the last time she saw him.

"What's going on?" she asked. "I thought bringing Sarith back to the real world would stop all of this. How is the beast still alive and so much bigger? There's no way she has magic in the real world. There's just no way."

"Cara, we made a terrible mistake. It wasn't Sarith that made and controlled the beast," Terrance said, looking deep into her eyes.

"Then who?"

"It's James."

Forty-Four

Woodrow's sword crashed against another. He swung just before his opponent and he felt the blade hit the animal's soft flesh. He went down. Woodrow darted to the left around him. Fighting was not something he wanted to do, but he knew there was no other way. Scanning the scene, he was looking for Cara. Her and Sarith were fighting near the bridge. He jumped and dodged the others as he went. He darted around the bridge and approached from the far side.

When he saw Cara fall onto her back, he tossed her his sword and gave her a quick nod. He knew she was the only one who could finish this war.

Across the battleground, the war raged on. The cries of victory and defeat filled the air. The smell of blood mixed with sweat was palpable.

His eyes scanned for any sign of his friends. He had to know if they were alright. He saw Cynthia battling a fox, while the mayor was near the front of the battle, fighting another lion.

His heartbeat quickened. He hadn't seen James yet. When the battle first began, he was further down the line, saying he wanted to spread the powerful fighters apart. He hadn't seen him in far too long. He scanned again and again. Woodrow ran into the battle, grabbed a sword of a fallen soldier and started swinging at those who challenged him. He wasn't about to lose his best friend.

"James!" he called, but his voice was lost in the sounds of battle. He ran back towards the forest, wondering if perhaps he had met his end early in the battle. He scanned the tree line and saw a flash out of the corner of his eye. It was golden fur, just like James's.

He ran, jumping over the casualties he came to. Another flash of fur. It was heading deeper into the forest.

The tunnels, Woodrow thought.

He followed and watched as it disappeared near an old tree. Woodrow quickly approached and took a deep breath. He didn't know these tunnels as well as James did, but he could get around. Knocking on a nearby root of a tree, a door opened. He jumped down into it and fell to the floor below.

He landed on his feet and slowly stood, waiting while his eyes adjusted to the lower lighting.

"Hurry!" He heard someone say. It echoed around him. It was coming down the tunnel to his left.

He turned and quietly made his way down there. It sounded close. He couldn't be sure, though. He peeked his head around the corner of the tunnel and saw four foxes.

One of them had a typewriter, while the other two had the enchanted boxes. Woodrow stood shocked for a moment. No one ever moved them, especially without a supervisor.

"Is that all of them?" he heard the one holding the typewriter say.

"Yes."

"Positive?"

"What's taking so long?" He heard another one. Only this time, he knew that voice. Chills washed over his body. It was James.

What was he doing? Woodrow wondered.

"Just making sure we have them all." He heard one of them say.

"You better be sure that we do," James said. "If they get their hands on even one of these, they can cause havoc. And I will hold the three of you personally responsible. And trust me, I will make it so that you will have wished you followed my directions. I will make you smell the roses your family brings you in the hospital out of your ears."

"Yes, sir."

Woodrow was stunned. He had never heard his friend talk like that before. He forgot all about hiding and took a step out towards them.

"What—?" was all Woodrow got out before the three foxes he didn't know took off running, while James looked him dead in the eye. They stood there looking at each other. Woodrow didn't know what to do. Why was he moving everything? What did he have planned and why hadn't Woodrow seen it coming?

"What are you doing?" Woodrow said when his voice finally came back out.

"You shouldn't have come here," James said.

Woodrow took another step closer.

"What are you doing with that typewriter? And the enchanted boxes?" He took another step and shot a look into the Dream Writing room. The tables were all over-turned, the curtains covering the clay walls had been ripped and now hung at odd angles, while the typewriters had been cleared out.

"Do you really think this was all about Sarith?" James scoffed. "Oh, silly Woodrow."

"But, how? Why?"

"There are so many things you don't know. So many things."

"What are you going to do with them?" Woodrow asked, his voice quivering.

"Something I should have done a long time ago."

James cuffed him ruthlessly. He heard the impact through his skull and it rattled his teeth. Woodrow flew back and hit the wall behind him. The world went dark.

Forty-Five

Cynthia knocked on Woodrow's door for the tenth time that day. He has been missing since the battle ended, and no one has found him amongst the casualties. Worry was setting in.

Terrance walked up behind her, smoothing out his mane.

"I've been wondering where he is too," he said. She turned around and looked up into his enormous eyes.

"You're the mayor. You've got authority. Can't we go in and see if there are any clues where he's gone?" Cynthia said.

"I think it's probably safe to say he's with James," Terrance replied.

"Woodrow's not a villain, if that's what you're suggesting. He was — no, is a good person," Cynthia said.

"Listen, I'm just saying that he's not around anymore and maybe that's because he's joined the other side...

259

Although maybe they took him? That's always a chance too." He looked at Cynthia and saw the desperation in her eyes. "Fine, but you better not tell anyone we did this."

Terrance grabbed the door handle and, using all his weight, knocked against the door three times before the wood frame finally gave. The door crashing to the floor and he stumbled in.

The air was stale and smelt like decay. Cynthia came up behind him and gasped. She reached over and turned on the lights to be sure of what she was really seeing.

The once lush plants that surrounded Woodrow's home were all dead.

"He's only been missing for two days! These plants wouldn't have died that quickly," Cynthia said, walking up closer to the one on the kitchen windowsill.

There they remained, their shapes still holding together. But as she reached out and touched it, the plant quickly turned to ash and fell to the sill. She looked down at her hand and it was covered in ash that smeared when she tried to rub it off. Like a chain reaction, she watched as the rest of the plants around the room dissolved and fell. Clouds of ash bellowed into the air, making Cynthia cough and quickly she covered her face.

"Terrance, something is very wrong," Cynthia said, looking up at him.

He grabbed her hand and as they turned to leave. Cynthia took one last look around and, with a heavy heart, stepped back over the bits of broken door and into the fresh air.

* * *

Terrance and Cynthia entered the tunnels and made their way towards the Dream Writing room. They turned down the hall towards it and stopped dead in their tracks. The door was wide open and just before it was what looked like a pile of cloth. Terrance looked at Cynthia and motioned for her to wait while he approached. It was a pile of clothing, and he instantly knew who they belonged to. They had been Woodrow's. But something was different about them. It was like he had fallen and the clothes melted off his body. Cynthia came over, flashlight in hand, and shone it towards the clothing. In the spots that would have been his body were now piles of ash. Cynthia stumbled back and met Terrance's eyes before pushing past him into the Dream Writing room.

What once was an elegant room was now a shadow of its former self. Darkness hung around the room like cobwebs, blurring the corners and giving the room a chill.

All over the room was nothing but chaos. The tables were now overturned and the chairs smashed. The curtains that once hung around the room, giving it a warm feeling and making it elegant, now hung at weird angles.

Neither one of them spoke as they checked room after room. The destruction was heartbreaking, and Cynthia almost couldn't stand it. Although she had never worked here, she had visited and watched all the great things they had done. They had helped people understand their true passions and gave them hope in their lives.

She couldn't take it anymore. Each step became more difficult than the last. It was too painful to see and she knew they would have to go back and tell the others what had happened. If James could do this, then who knows what else he might try to do.

"Can we get out of here?" Cynthia asked, looking at Terrance. He looked just as broken about the scene as she was.

He murmured in agreement but barely acknowledged her. As they were about to leave the room, Cynthia stopped herself and scanned the room once more. The far corner where the darkness seemed to consume the room the most was the spot where James had set up his desk. She remembered it well. He had made it quite comfortable, so when he didn't have to be comforting the others, he would have a small retreat that he could go back to. It was the one place he said he could collect his thoughts and gain strength to help those writing. The corner drew her over.

Someone had thrown James's favourite chair under the table where the enchanted boxes used to be. Cynthia reached down and pulled the chair out and looked it over. Somehow, they hadn't fully destroyed it. She put it back where it had sat for years, and let herself sit. The chair groaned loudly in protest, but held. Before her, she could still picture the other animals typing away: some enjoying what they were writing, while others grimaced. With every grimace, James would have walked over and placed a hand on their shoulder to remind them they weren't alone. She let the image fall from her thoughts. That wasn't the real James. Everything they thought they had known about him was a lie and somehow he had done a good job hiding his real side.

What parts of James had been real, if any? Cynthia wondered as she sat there, her hind paw kicking nervously, stirring up a cloud of dust. Terrance was sitting on the floor, unmoving. She wished Terrance would come over and comfort her with some words, but she could see that emotions were overwhelming him as well. Maybe he was thinking the same thing she was. Cynthia let herself cry, tears falling to the ground. Her frame shook and her heart wept. Someone that had been such a huge part of their town for so long was now only a memory, even though he still existed. Nothing would ever be the same again.

She wept for the town. She wept for those whom they wrote the dreams for, but mostly, she wept for the friendship she knew was lost forever.

She remained there, shoulders hunched until she finally felt like there was nothing else left inside of her. Terrance had come over at one point and crouched beside her but he let her weep. She wiped her eyes and hung her head. Opening her eyes, she saw the scattered pattern her tears had made on the ground like raindrops fallen from the sky.

Taking a few deep breaths, she took a last look around.

"You okay?" Terrance asked, cradling her arm in his, about to help her up.

She looked down, bracing herself to stand, but at her feet, something glimmered. Her tears had cleared the debris off of something. She reached down and wiped at the spot and from the dirt she found a single letter 'W' looking back at her.

"Terrance?"

He looked down too and saw it. Cynthia reached down and pulled it out of the hard dirt floor. It was from a Royal typewriter. She recognized the key from the typewriter that James had always used since the dream-writing room first came to be. Those were the best days the room had ever seen. There was energy in the air. That was before Sarith had come. That was before all of this had started.

Still bent over, her eyes lifted and looked under the table in front of her. Hidden under it was the typewriter this key had come from. Gingerly, she pulled it out and looked it over. The keys were smashed and shattered, while the type bars were bent at obscure angles. The casing was crushed, pieces sprayed around it like candy from a piñata.

Carefully, she picked it up, balancing the dangling pieces in her small hands. Terrance took it. The only reason they would have left it behind was if they either didn't know they had missed it, or maybe they believed it wasn't fixable. But perhaps they were wrong.

Cynthia followed Terrance towards the doorway and out the door. This time, she didn't even want to look back. Now was the time to move forward.

Forty-Six

"What do you mean it's James?" Cara asked, as she and Melissa followed Terrance through the tunnels.

He led them as quickly as he could and stopped just short of the Dream Writing room.

"Where are we?" Melissa asked, looking at the door, fear deeply etched in her face.

"Terrance, why are we at James's place? Why are we in the Dream Writing room?" Cara asked, turning her back to the door and looking at him dead in the eye.

He pointed to the clothes on the floor in front of them, and Cara knelt down to examine them. A chill swept through her as she took in the frayed edges and simple material. Woodrow had chosen a simple woven shirt, something lightweight, so he wouldn't get too hot under the armour. This was definitely his. Dust fell from it and to the floor. She put it down and rubbed her fingers together. The grey dust smeared over her skin like butter.

"Woodrow," she breathed and let herself look back at Terrance.

He cleared her throat before finally speaking. Even after that, Cara could hear the quiver in his voice.

"Yes. Before we wrote you that dream, we came down here to see what we could find. With Woodrow missing, the only place we could think of him being would be down here. Maybe he was trying to save the Dream Writing room or something. But that's all we found.

"Cara, that's all that's left. He's turned to ash," Terrance said, somehow looking smaller than he had just a moment ago.

"What?" she asked, backing away from the clothes. She looked at her ash-streaked fingers and wiped them on the wall beside her.

"We went to his house to find him, and instead we found all his plants had turned to ash. We knew something was wrong. Then, we came here and found that. He's gone," Cynthia added, her long ears hanging low.

The world spun. She reached out to balance herself. Melissa grabbed her elbow and helped her remain standing on legs now turned to pudding.

Melissa looked at Terrance, and she shot him a questioning look.

Cara looked at them and motioned for him to tell Melissa. If she was going to be here, she had to know what was going on.

As Terrance told Melissa about the fight between Sarith and Cara, Cara could feel Melissa's eyes on her. Melissa had never given her any credit before. She had never seen her as anything but that nerd that they bullied. But as the story unfolded, Cara saw something that surprised her.

Across Melissa's face was the look of embarrassment and discomfort. Maybe, just for once, Melissa saw that the person she had been bullying all this time was actually capable of so much more.

Cara stood up tall. When he finished the retelling of everything they had gone through, he finally turned the door and slowly pushed it open.

Cara took a few steps inside and gasped at the ruins left behind.

"We don't know exactly what happened, but we think Woodrow came down here either during or after the battle and ran into James. We think James did that to him. And that would have been when he took all the typewriters."

"After you both left, the armies stopped fighting. They saw their leaders were gone and we didn't think we'd ever see you again. So we all left. Even the beast. We all had assumed it was to die. How could he live on without his creator? Only somehow he did. And not only that, he had gotten bigger. That's when we knew something more was going on."

"But I just... But why? Why would he do all this?" Cara asked.

"That's what we need to find out," Terrance said.

"Wait, how did you manage to get a hold of me?"

"Well, after we couldn't find Woodrow, Cynthia and I came here and looked around. We found Woodrow's armour and clothes in a pile outside the room, covered in ash like you saw. Then inside the room, we found what was left of a single typewriter. The thing was literally in shambles. I figured it was a long shot that we could fix it, but we had to try. Just as I was about to leave the Dream Writing room, I spotted a dormouse cowering near the doorway. He was trembling. I knew pretty quickly that he wasn't a part of James's crew. Cynthia scooped him up and brought him, and the typewriter remains, back to her place. The townsfolk we showed the typewriter to tried to do something with it, but no one had any luck. But we kept trying. We figured it was the only way to get a hold of you. How else could we possibly communicate with the human world?

"And after everything, and finding out the beast was still alive and doing better than ever, we were scared. We had to tell you what was going on," Terrance said, walking into the room.

"When the dormouse's nerves finally settled, he came around to the table Cynthia had set the typewriter on and looked it over. He climbed inside and got to work adjusting the type arms, the casing was coming together, and he was hammering something inside. So, we just left him to it. Every few hours, Cynthia came back to him with food and water. Many hours later, he came out and the whole thing was back together. Sure, the casing was still missing pieces because we hadn't gotten them all, but somehow, he made it work.

"That's how we were able to contact you," he continued. "Without it, I don't think you would have ever known. We think James is shielding you from all the bad dreams and only giving you good ones at this point so he can stay in charge. He knows you're the only one that can stop him now. Finding that typewriter was a stroke of luck that we needed. He's got an army now. I wonder if that's why he did all this, was to gain the army."

"Where are the other typewriters?" Cara asked.

"Somewhere in his care. We don't know exactly yet, but we know it's pretty close. We can hear the beast constantly, but he leaves us alone. It's because if they control the typewriters and the dreams, then they don't have to force us to do it anymore."

Cara just shook her head. If all this was true and that James was truly the one behind it all along, then what else did he have planned? Why did the nightmares really mean so much to him?

Cara walked back over, her shoulder aching in pain.

"But my shoulder. How could I possibly defeat him with my shoulder like this?" Cara asked. She held her arm close. "And why would he wait until Sarith left to take over?"

"Sarith is human. She's stronger than us, remember? He probably had to wait until she was gone before he could take over. But how he's gotten this strong, I don't know.

"But for now, we need to get you looked over and we'll go from there. We have an advantage now. He doesn't know you are here," Terrance said, coming back over to her.

"But where is everyone?"

"In our new home."

Forty-Seven

Terrance led her and Melissa back through the tunnels and they continued in silence for what felt like an eternity.

"It's okay," Cara said, holding back a step to match Melissa's pace.

Ahead they heard rushing water and as they approached, the mist fell on her skin and chilled her. She looked over at Melissa and saw she felt the same way. They turned a corner and stopped. They were behind a wall of water rushing down past an opening in the wall.

"Where are we?" Cara shouted, covering her ears as best as she could.

Terrance motioned for her to follow him through a small doorway to the right of the water.

"Be careful!" he shouted, pointing down a slick staircase. The mist cast a shining film over everything. Cara held onto the crude handrail as they went down the steep incline. Her feet slipped but she held tight to the railing to not fall. Not daring to take her eyes off her unsteady feet, she used her free hand and wiped the water off her face, trying to see through the mist, but it was impossible. The stairs led them down beside the water and veered away from it and to the right. As they walked away from the water and mist, Cara could see they were heading down towards a small shoreline of what she assumed was a lake that the falls poured into. Her feet sunk into the wet sand and she finally looked up and took in the sight around her.

Small homes were all over the shoreline, each made of stones and wood. The structures were erected quickly and crudely, but they did the job. A few of her friends were milling about, some cooking over small fires in open spaces between the homes, while others sat and chatted. She smiled, seeing Cynthia sitting and talking at a table. She was surrounded by townsfolk that she had seen but didn't know well. Cynthia reached over to a pot that was sitting on the fire nearby, ready to give it a stir, but stopped midway. Her jaw flew open, and she dropped the spoon. A friend sitting next to her stopped mid-sentence to follow her gaze.

Cara laughed and waved before running towards her. Cynthia ran and met her halfway. Cynthia's arms wrapped around her and gave her a fierce hug. She winced slightly against the shoulder and she quickly let go.

"Sorry, your shoulder. Are you okay? It's so good to see you!"

"I'm okay. It's fine," Cara said.

"I never thought I'd see you again," Cynthia said, looking the rest of her over. "The typewriter worked!"

"It did! I got that dream and I knew something was wrong."

Cynthia opened her mouth to say something, but stopped and looked over Cara's head at Melissa.

Cara followed his gaze and chuckled. Melissa stood at the bottom of the staircase and waited.

"Where are my manners?" Cara went back to Melissa and gently hooked her good arm into Melissa's and pulled her over.

"Don't worry," Cara whispered into Melissa's ear. She could tell that Melissa was amazed by the sight, just like she had been the first time she saw all the animals doing all the things humans could do.

"This is Melissa," she said when they approached Cynthia. Now, around her, a crowd had formed, all of them looking in shock to see two humans.

"We're here to help," Cara said to the hopeful faces around her.

Terrance walked up behind them and joined the circle. She could tell that he was pleased she was back. They walked away from the crowd and to a quieter spot, away from the river and along the mountains on the other side.

"Terrance, I don't understand how we missed this," Cara said as they walked.

"He had us all fooled. That's really all I can say. I didn't see it coming either. He is definitely not the person I thought he was," Terrance said.

They headed back over to the fire and sat down around it.

Terrance carefully scooped out steaming carrot stew into bowls and passed them around.

Between bites, the animals told her everything that had happened once she and Sarith had left the battlefield. Cara could see Melissa's discomfort, hearing it all and knowing it was her mother. She tried to catch Melissa's attention, but Melissa kept herself turned away.

Cynthia and Terrance took turns explaining how James had attacked the city. They had planned to try to find him, but before they could, James, along with the beast and his army, attacked. They injured and killed dozens, but many more got away in time. After that, they went into hiding and came to the falls. It wasn't the easiest place to live, but they were close to drinking water and would be alright for the time being.

"We want to fight him, but after seeing how big the beast has gotten, we really don't think we'll defeat him, which is why we had hoped the typewriter would work. And brought a friend?" Terrance said, eyeing up Melissa.

"I'm not sure we'd call each other friends exactly," Cara said. Finally Melissa turned back towards the conversation. "But we're on better terms now, I think?" she said, asking Melissa if she agreed.

"I'm the bully," Melissa said flatly. "She probably told you about me. I was the one that started it all. I'm the one that did that to her arm. Well, I didn't actually do it, but I told the other girl to do it." Melissa stood up to leave.

"Sit, please," Cara said, grabbing her hand.

"Why? So I can feel worse than I already do?"

"No, because you can make things better by helping us," Cara said.

"But my mom," Melissa said, her voice dropping in volume.

"I know, but make things right. Make them right here. Help me, help my friends and let's at least make their world better. We can figure everything else out about home at home," Cara said.

Melissa took a deep breath and sat back down.

"Your mom?" Cynthia asked.

Melissa and Cara exchanged a look but Cara put her hands up. She didn't want to be the one to tell them if Melissa didn't want it.

"My mom," Melissa said, pushing a stray hair away from her face, "is Sarith."

They all stopped and looked at her, unsure of what to say. Cynthia and the others turned to Terrance, and he straightened himself out. He motioned for her to continue. She really didn't know what else to say.

"I think it might be partly my fault that she was so mad. We had this big fight before she left. I was horrible to her and I think that maybe it's my fault," Melissa said.

"I'm sure it wasn't," Terrance said, coming over closer to her.

"But I was," Melissa said. "And I've been horrible to everyone around me because I've been so mad about her being gone. But I'd like to try and be better from now on." She glanced at Cara. "If you'll let me, I'd like to help."

"We would love to have you. Especially since I'm not too sure what all I can do with this shoulder like this," Cara said, holding her arm close again.

"I think we can help you with that." Cynthia rose and crossed over the river before returning with the doctor. He had his medical bag with him and he grinned when he saw Cara. She hadn't met him before, but she had heard about him. Having the gift of healing, he rarely needed to use medicine. Most was done by magic. He looked at her eye, then slowly took the sling off her shoulder.

"I'm Dr. Rogan. It's a pleasure to meet you after all of this."

She grimaced slightly against the pain of moving her shoulder and bit her lip. She held her breath until he let go.

"I appreciate you looking at it," Cara said.

"What did the other doctor say?"

"That it's bad. Separated, but should heal in a few weeks."

Dr. Rogan put his hands above her shoulder and closed his eyes. Cara could see the air above it swirl and after a few moments, she could feel the warmth seeping into her skin. It actually felt great. He stayed that way for a while, and her shoulder got warmer and warmer, but never too hot. She thought she could feel the tension in it falling away and for a brief moment, she thought it might be getting better. The doctor stopped and she opened her eyes.

"Try it."

Cara carefully went to lift it, but quickly the pain overcame her again. She could feel the pain shooting down her arm and through her chest. A yelp escaped her lips and she collapsed back onto the chair.

"It didn't work?" He seemed genuinely surprised, but shook it off.

"Let me try again." Dr. Rogan sat down beside her this time and put his hands right on her shoulder. He took his time and she felt an even stronger intensity in her shoulder and it radiated out through her body. She gasped slightly and he gave her shoulder a last nudge and pulled his hands away. He took a few deep breaths himself, before motioning for her to try again.

She carefully and slowly lifted her arm again, but pain shot up again.

Melissa stood and walked away. Cara watched her go but stayed where she was.

"This has never happened before," Dr. Rogan said, clearly confused.

"It's probably because I'm human."

"Well," he said, "I can give you something for pain if you want, but I'm not doing any good here."

Dismay clouded her face, but she thanked him as he walked back the way he came.

"Now what am I supposed to do?" she asked, still watching Melissa.

"I don't know. For now, we'll eat," Terrance said, motioning to the fire before them.

"I'll be right back," she whispered to Terrance before she walked over to Melissa and stood beside her quietly for a moment.

Melissa had walked back over to the falls and stood in the thick mist, letting it drench her. "I'm really sorry about everything," Melissa said without turning.

"I know you are. I'm going to be fine," Cara said, hoping it sounded like it in her voice.

"But how are you going to help your friends? How are you going to stop this James character from actually destroying everything? You say that when you had magic here earlier, that somehow you saved everyone, but now, you can't. And you can't expect me to be able to do anything. I just got here and I don't have a black belt or anything," Melissa said, finally turning to face Cara.

"They have a plan. Let's hear it out before we jump to any conclusions, okay?" Cara said.

Melissa agreed, and Cara put her hand on Melissa's shoulder. Suddenly, a pulse radiated out of them and rushed over everyone around them, putting out the campfires out and making them drop what they were holding.

"What was that?" Melissa asked, eyes wide.

Cara turned to her and let out a holler.

She ran back to Terrance who had seen the pulse too, and together they started talking over one another in excitement.

They didn't have time to teach Melissa magic, but the power of two would be more than they needed to defeat James.

Forty-Eight

"The good thing is, we have the element of surprise," Cynthia said, after most of the town had turned in for the night. The stars shone brightly overhead and in numbers that Cara had never seen before. She always loved the stars. The wide open sheet of them across the sky always made her feel so small, but also at peace. She couldn't believe that tomorrow would be their last day here and that there would likely be a large amount of bloodshed.

"What's the plan?" Melissa asked, moving closer to the fire as the air cooled off around them.

"We know he's at the castle and has what used to be Sarith's army working for him now," Cynthia said.

"I don't understand how they could possibly want to do anything for him, especially after seeing what all he's done," Cara said.

"They're probably scared stiff, or maybe they just are so brainwashed at this point," Cynthia suggested.

"I guess so..."

"Either way, we," Cynthia said as she flipped open a notepad, "have a plan. James doesn't know that we have a typewriter. He only knows that we have moved and are staying away. As you know, we don't have dreams. Now that you are here and we have the strength of a human on our side, well, two actually," she said, looking over at Melissa, "we know how to get him to come out of the castle. Hopefully, then we'll be able to defeat him."

Cara put her glass down gently. James had been a friend of hers. The thought that he was now the one behind all of this seemed impossible.

Cynthia put a paw on her hand.

"I know this is a lot to take in but at least we have a plan, right? We're going to write him a dream. No, a nightmare. We'll make it something he'll know isn't from one of his own writers. We'll include you and maybe something to do with his ruin. Once he wakes up, he'll probably come and find us. And we'll be waiting. I think we should tell him in the dream that he needs to come to the field where you first learned you had magic. That way, he's out of his comfort zone of the castle, and he can't surprise us with any extra attack equipment."

"That sounds good," Cara said, thinking it over. That would be better for them. It was a neutral spot, so there was no chance of James having an upper hand.

"I'll type out the dream outside there in the field because I bet once he has the dream, he'll come for us," Cynthia said.

"With the army," Cara said.

"With the army," Cynthia agreed. "But we'll be ready for him."

"Then we'll attack," Cara whispered.

"He's going to be strong. A lot stronger than we've ever seen him before, but I know we can do this. I've already got volunteers in place that want to go with us and the blacksmiths have been working on additional armour since we called you back."

Cara pictured all those animals surrounding her, covered in armour, waiting for a battle that could end their lives. It made her scared, but also relieved she didn't have to do this alone. And with Melissa here, even if she didn't have any magic, they could join forces just by holding hands and that would increase her strength, maybe even double it.

James didn't stand a chance.

Forty-Nine

Though it hadn't been too long since she first learned to use her magic in this field, it now felt like an eternity had passed. The expression on General Barabus's face when he found out she had magic and could harm him was unforgettable.

The field was empty except for Melissa, who stood beside her. Cynthia appeared from one of the tunnels, the typewriter in hand, and came up beside her.

"Ready?" Cynthia asked, looking at Cara with a hint of a smile.

"I never thought I'd have to do this again. I thought Sarith was going to be it." Cara shook her head in disbelief.

"We all did." Cynthia took a deep breath.

"Let's do this," Cara said.

Cynthia put the typewriter down on the grass and began working. Her fingers flew as each key slapped the paper.

When she was done, she pulled the paper out and put it and the typewriter down. They knew it wouldn't take long before James came out. Now it was just a waiting game.

Fifty

James woke up with a start, his eyes darting around, trying to process what he had just seen and where he was. He looked around the room and saw he was definitely still in bed. Wiping his face and beads of sweat somehow were forming on his nose. He didn't understand. As a dog, he never sweat, yet, as he pulled his paw away, there it was: the moisture that made his fur damp. He threw back the covers on his bed and swung his feet around. He took several deep breaths. What had woken him up so abruptly? He had never had this before.

Then it came back. Flashes and images of him out in a field. But not just any field. As the pictures became clearer, it came to him: it was the field Cara had first figured out she had magic. He was surrounded by the others: the ones that he turned against. But what were they doing? They were closing in. He was alone. There was no way out. He could feel his breathing getting faster as the images became clearer. He felt the hot breath of them on his back and he turned to see Cara, standing there smiling at him, her white teeth sharp and dagger-like. She raised a sword at him. He went to raise his, but saw he wasn't holding a sword but a notebook. He opened it up and inside all he found was a single line that read, "I'm coming for you."

He dropped it and looked up again to see Cara right in front of him. With one swift movement, she swung her sword, and it hit him on his left side, the astonishing pain shooting up him and instantly he was awake.

He forced himself to stand and took a few wobbly steps past the bed and to the bathroom. He splashed some water on his face and looked at his reflection. The images of the dream were fading, but he still saw the fear in his eyes. As he towel dried his face, reality hit. He had had a nightmare. But no one had dreams in this world. Someone had written him a dream. But who would dare? He threw the towel down and stormed out of his room. As he crossed the castle, his nails clicking on the solid stone, he felt not only determination to find out who would dare do this but also ready to start a fight. This was not acceptable.

He came up to the wing of the castle they had moved the Dream Writing rooms to. The rooms were smaller, so they needed more of them. Even outside the room, he could hear the crashing of keys hitting the paper. He threw open the door and instantly everyone inside stopped.

"Who did it!" he said, more as a command than a question.

The animals looked at him with fear etched in their eyes.

"Who!" He said louder.

From the other room, General Barabus came out, confusion covering his face.

"James, what's wrong?" he asked, stopping in front of him.

"The nightmare. Who did it?" James said, his eyes darting around.

"I'm sorry, James, but I don't know what you're talking about," General Barabus said.

"Oh, is that so? Well, someone in one of these rooms wrote me a nightmare. Did you really think that was a wise choice?" James looked each one of them in the eyes, most showed fear, some were shaking.

"Is this true?" The General asked, looking at those at the typewriters.

They all shook their heads, and some even threw their hands up in a questioning way.

"Enough! When I find out who did this, they will be hanged!" James shouted.

He darted to the first typist and ripped the sheet out of the typewriter and looked it over. This dream had another person's name on it.

He went to the next, then the next, ripping sheet after sheet out, finding nothing to show they were being written about him. He ran into the next room and continued, ripping sheet after sheet after sheet out of the typewriters, throwing them on the ground when he saw someone else's name.

The General followed him at a distance, reaching down every so often to check out the page James had just dropped, ensuring it had nothing to do with him. And seeing it didn't, he let it fall back onto the floor.

James felt his pulse quicken with each sheet ripped out of each typewriter and finding absolutely nothing to show that any of these were about him. He finally got to the last one and stopped.

"You," he said to the fox, sitting in the chair. "That only makes sense."

The fox was shaking but shook his head no. As James pulled the last sheet out, he saw the one thing that he wasn't prepared for: someone else's name.

How could that be? James staggered back and crumbled the sheet in his hand before throwing it into the fox's face. The fox flinched, but stayed where he was. James stumbled out of the room and back into the hallway, where he leaned on the wall for a moment, his thoughts racing.

"Sir?" General Barabus said.

James stood and rubbed his head.

"What was… what happened there?" General Barabus asked cautiously.

"I woke up from a nightmare," James said, finally looked at the General.

"But how?"

"You tell me!" James shouted. "I figured someone was doing it to me as a joke. Now I'm not so sure."

"I don't think I'm following. If they didn't do this as a joke, then how? And what did you dream about that made you so panicked?" General Barabus asked.

"It was about Cara, and her… coming back," he said, deciding the General didn't need to know the full dream.

"Cara? But she left. Why would you dream about her? You don't think... she wouldn't have come back, would she?" he asked cautiously.

Suddenly, it hit James. The idea that she was back wasn't something that should have surprised him. Of course she could come back, but unless she knew something was wrong, she wouldn't have. And the only way that she would have is if someone outside this castle had a typewriter to contact her. Woodrow's surprised face when he saw James and the others taking and moving all the things out of the old Dream Writing room suddenly came to mind. They had been interrupted by Woodrow. Was it possible one had gotten missed? James pushed past the General and back into the writing room. All the typing ceased again as they turned to face him.

"You, you and you," he said, pointing at the foxes who had helped him that day, "come outside. Now."

They followed him into the hall and stood against the stone wall. He could see them shaking, and not just because of how cold it was out here.

"Did you three actually double-check the old Dream Writing room when we invaded it, making sure you got everything?"

They exchanged looks but all of them nodded in unison.

"Are you absolutely sure?" James growled.

The one opened his mouth to talk, but the other two shot him looks that clearly said for him to shut it again.

"What's your name again?" James leaned into the one fox that had opened his mouth, blocking his view of his two friends.

"Jonathan," he stammered.

"Ah, yes, Jonathan. That's right. Tell me, Jonathan, did you all triple-check the room or did you just do a quick sweep and hope it was enough? It looks like you wanted to get something off your chest."

"We, uh, I mean, I uh…" his voice trailed off.

"You checked, but you didn't double-check, did you?"

"Jon!" his one friend said, before the General grabbed and shoved him against the wall.

"I see. I think I understand what happened here. Thanks, gentlemen. General, you can take it from here, right?"

He nodded, but James didn't look back to watch. He had already turned and was walking away.

Behind him, he heard the cries of the three of them as the General's fist crashed against them, sending them to the floor in agony.

Fifty-One

James quickly walked through the castle and out to the side courtyard where the troops were training. His blood boiled.

She's back, he thought.

Since Cara had left, he hadn't spoken to any of the townsfolk, which was more than fine with him. He didn't need to answer to anyone, especially someone like Cynthia, Terrance, or any of them, for that matter. He was in charge and that's what he always wanted. No one was going to spoil this for him now, not even Cara.

He stopped just short of where the army was doing drills and watched. The smell of determination and sweat filled the air.

Behind him, he heard the door to the castle close and General Barabus stopped short when seeing James, but came up beside him.

"I've taken care of those three," he said.

"Good. Prepare the army. We're leaving. Remember that field where you learnt that Cara has magic? We're going there. Only I want you and the army to stay out of sight until I signal."

"Yes sir. We can be ready in the next few minutes."

James watched as the General headed back over to his troops and gave a command. And like a well-oiled clock, the entire troop turned and got the rest of their gear and armour on. The sound rattled in James's ears and stung, but he only grinned through it. It might hurt to hear, but it was also the sound of a coming victory, one he would enjoy every moment of.

* * *

He arrived at the field alone, waiting for her to show her face. He was almost excited about this battle. This one would taste as sweet as honey and be just as smooth. He would keep his army hidden and, at just the right moment, bring them up like a swarm of locusts and crush this simpleton before she knew what was happening.

He laughed at the very thought of this sweet victory. He knew she was nearby, if not already here. But either way, he would let her make her entrance and let her think she had the upper hand, for now.

* * *

The moment he laughed, Cara stepped out into the field but kept her distance. She walked out into the centre of the field, only Cynthia with her. James stood alone.

"I knew it was you," he said, looking around.

She took another step closer and paused. She didn't want to get too close to this creature that she now barely recognized. His fur coat was no longer the light golden colour it had been. Now it was so dark and coppery that it almost looked chocolate brown. He was somehow taller and his eyes no longer had the sparkle they once had. Now they wreaked of darkness. She couldn't believe this was the animal that at one time she had trusted more than anyone else in the world.

"And where is our other friend, the one that found the typewriter?" James asked, his voice coming out more like a growl.

Cynthia, who had been behind Cara, stepped to the side so that James could see her but remained behind.

James looked at Cara and scoffed.

"So, you came back after all."

She watched his eyes scan her too, and he laughed.

"You're not looking so hot there, Cara," he snarled at her. James slowly walked over.

Cara watched him approach, but held her ground. He slowly circled her. James stopped right in front of her and looked her dead in the eye.

"Why?" she asked.

"Why did I do all of this?" He laughed. His mouth turned into a wicked smile that scared her.

"Why does anyone do bad things? Because it's fun," he hissed, chuckling to himself.

"But you hurt so many people. You've caused so much pain. You've terrified people all in the name of fun? I don't believe it," Cara said.

"Well, it is!" He shouted, his eyes wide. Cara jumped at the sound.

"My life was so boring," he said, emphasizing the last word, "before I started all this and I was so mad at what I was told I had to do day in and day out. Stay in a room with typewriters, watch the others do all the fun work by typing. You could go crazy doing all that everyday forever." He moved his hands in large circles beside his head. "And I guess some would say I did go crazy." He laughed half-heartedly.

Cara watched as he walked around behind her again. His circling was making her nervous.

"My dream was to garden, but life didn't give me that, now did it?"

"But you could have! You didn't have to do all this!" Cara said, turning to watch him walk back in front of her.

He stopped and walked up to her, leaving only inches between them. She could feel the heat of his breath on her and it made her tremble.

"Really?" He stared at her a moment before reaching down and grabbing a wildflower that was at Cara's feet. He held it up to her and watched as it quickly wilted, then browned and turned to ash and fell from his hand. He hunched his shoulders, stretching out the muscles and rubbing his paws together. The final bits of ash fell to the world below.

"Maybe that's because you're bad now," she said.

James moved his head from side to side, cracking his neck, the evil grimace sending more waves of discomfort through her.

"Oh, I've always been bad," he hissed. "But now that Woodrow is gone, I guess you could argue that I'm just pure evil now."

"What?" she asked, her heartbeat quickening at her friend's name.

"You didn't see his remains?"

"Yes, but—"

"I'm glad to be rid of him, too. It was so awful having to be nice," James laughed.

"What did you do to him?"

"Woodrow? Oh, I destroyed him," he said, shaking his head, but flashing his teeth in a devilish grin. "I'm surprised you didn't realize this sooner, though. I guess you're not as quick as I thought... He was a manifestation of my good side. All my kindness, joy, and all those other horrible emotions are what made him up. I channeled all of that and made him so I wouldn't have to feel all those things," James said. He rubbed his fingers together like he was feeling the ashy remains of Woodrow, like Cara had before.

"Now that the good side of me doesn't exist anymore, neither does he."

Cara took a step back, stunned. But somehow it all made sense.

"If the beast was a manifestation of Sarith's anger, then I guess I shouldn't be surprised that Woodrow could be one of your goodness. But after Sarith left, the beast remained. He's yours, isn't he?" she asked, putting all the pieces together.

"She finally gets it people," he said, extending his arms out and turning to the crowd he was imagining around him. "I hated letting her take the credit, but I didn't want anyone to know the truth. Messing with everyone was just too much fun."

"But how?"

"Oh, that thing has been growing since I was young. One day it showed up after I had a huge anger blow out. It started so small, like a pesky little ant. And every time I did something out of anger, it got just a little bigger.

"And as my life slowly went a different way than expected and my anger grew, so did it. I actually got really good at hiding the little beast. But eventually it grew so large and it was getting restless. I couldn't keep it hidden anymore and a part of me was scared, too. Ha! Hard to believe that I was scared of it at one point. One day, I went to check on it and 'poof,'" he moved his hands like a cloud rising in the air and popping, "it was gone."

"It was my first ever moment of panic. I hated it. How you people live with that feeling is beyond me." He shook his head and flicked his eyes back at her.

"But lucky for me, that woman arrived. That wasn't planned but, what excellent timing."

"She was the perfect one to use to hide my true self. I was the one who started the rumour that the beast was hers and, like fools, everyone believed me. And why not? They hadn't known me to lie yet."

"How did you get her to go along with it all? Was she bad too?" Cara asked, not daring to take her eyes off him.

"Not at first, but I gave her the push she needed. I promised her power. You humans are so easy. Give you power and wealth, and you're set. She played along with it for a while and actually started to enjoy it. I got to the point where I had to do very little but enjoy the show. Then you," he hissed, "came and changed everything. If you had come when no one was around, then I could have taken care of you right away. That very public appearance," he sighed, "well, I had to figure out another way.

"So I lied. I had never planned to take you home. That day that we ran into the General? I orchestrated that. I told him to show up there. I sent you that nightmare to scare you into wanting to stay and actually challenge me, but like a coward, you ran. So, that night with the storm? Once I found out you were gone and, like I assumed correctly, trying to get home, I set up that lovely scene at the lake with all the fish. I hoped it would be enough to scare you from trying to get home again, and it was."

"But you killed all those animals!" Cara said, shivers washing over her again.

"Why yes I did," he said, bowing slightly.

Cara couldn't believe it. She watched as he looked down and brushed some dirt off the front of his shirt. Down near the bottom, he saw something sticky stuck to it and picked at it. When it finally came off, he examined it then flicked it off his fingers. He looked back at her, bored, waiting for her.

"Why would you want me to stay? It seems like you had everything planned," Cara said, feeling shaken at how little she knew about him.

"Oh I did. But staying on the sidelines for so long was driving me crazy. You can't understand how frustrated I was letting everyone think she was the real brains behind it all, when really it was me. All she did was show me how to control the beast. Once I had that figured out, I wanted back in the driver's seat.

"After the lake though, you followed the exact steps I hoped you would take. I acted like I didn't know about the twin attack, but that was so perfectly set up that it scared you into wanting to fight. And seeing the way you hurt the General? I knew we had you. You started working on your magic and since humans are the only ones that can defeat humans..." he let his voice trail off.

"You wanted me to defeat Sarith because you couldn't. You wanted to be in charge and take back control, but you could only do that if Sarith was gone. Which is why you wanted me to do it."

"By George, I think she has it!" James said, laughing again. He was enjoying this far too much.

"Anyway, you know the rest, I'm sure. I wasn't expecting you to actually come back. That was an interesting surprise. It's that damn typewriter they missed. I had you set up specifically to get good dreams so you wouldn't come back. Those moron soldiers. Anyway, they are being taken care of as we speak."

"So, what's the plan now? Just keep terrorising everyone?" Cara asked.

"Well, that was the plan. I guess it now includes defeating you first. Power is so intoxicating. I have never felt so strong in my life. It's exhilarating, really. I'm finally in charge.

"I guess now that you're here, you think you can stop me?" James asked, puffing out his chest. He took a deep breath and looked to the sky. Cara could tell he was enjoying this.

"I can't exactly walk away," Cara replied.

"Ah, the 'good guy' thought process always makes me laugh. You know you're no match for me, right? You might be human but that doesn't mean much anymore."

He looked behind himself and let out a loud whistle. Cara watched, but saw nothing at first. Then, the heads slowly emerged over the horizon and the army gathered behind him. Soon, the horizon was hidden behind the wall of creatures. She didn't expect so many. As they came closer, the clanging of their metal armour increased until it was so loud she covered her ears. James watched her and shook his head.

The army finally stopped and he took a step closer.

"There's no way you can beat me. I win," he smiled.

* * *

James watched her standing there alone. Noticing her nervous shake, He knew he had her. He would end her, then invade the town's new location and he would finally be in total control. It was everything he ever wanted, and he felt the waves of adrenaline pulsing through him.

He let his eyes wander to the troops behind him. They all stood ready. As he looked back at her, he saw a smile creep over her face. She stomped her foot three times and paused. He didn't understand. Then it hit him like a shot. Of course he knew. He knew better than anyone else and yet somehow he hadn't thought about it until now: the tunnels. The heads started coming up out of the ground like smiling zombies. One after another they emerged, armour in place, waiting for the attack. They surrounded Cara and stood tall.

When they finally stopped, James laughed again, only he wasn't feeling as confident now.

"You expect me to believe these simpletons are actually going to fight?" James called out to her. The crowd slowly parted and allowed Cara to come to the front. Some tried to stop her, but she raised her hand to stop them.

"James, your time has finally come to an end. They aren't going to let you, or anyone else for that matter, rule them ever again."

But she knew he wasn't believing her.

He sighed before shouting, "Go!"

This army raised their hands high and ran towards Cara and her army. Her army moved and the crashing of metal was almost deafening. Swords swung and Cara watched as some of her friends went down around her. She remained in her spot. James did the same. Around them was chaos, but they stayed. She watched him. She didn't even recognize him anymore. He took a step closer to her, someone bumping into him, but he just pushed them away. Cara took a step closer.

He charged and stopped right in front of her. He stood and pulled himself up to his full height, so they were looking eye-to-eye. She could feel his hot breath on her face as he came only inches away from her face.

"You're finished," he hissed.

He grabbed her and put one paw on her chest and the other around her back, holding her tight.

Cara didn't understand. What was he thinking he could do to her? She knew that as a human she had more power than he did, but as he stood there, she felt a burning sensation starting in her chest. Looking down, her clothes started to brown and burn. She was confused. Then, the pain took over. It was intense. She cried out. A few animals around her stopped to see what was going on. The pain intensified and she could barely think.

She heard her name called out, but it sounded like it was a million miles away. Was she dying?

She pushed as hard as she could against him, trying to make him back off, but she couldn't. With her arm injured, she wasn't strong enough. She opened her eyes again and saw that her army was trying to pull him off, but they couldn't.

Then, clarity swept over her like she hadn't had in a very long time. He was using her magic and strength against her. And in that moment, she understood that not only was her life about to end, but that it was about to end at the hand of a bully. She always thought Melissa would be the one. That word, that simple word, bully, echoed in her head over and over as the pain got so bad she could barely breathe.

She felt herself get angry. Almost irrationally angry. She would not have her life end at the hand of a bully. That was not the end of her story. It would not be the end of her.

She opened her eyes again and pushed with everything in her. Suddenly, he was off her and tumbling backwards.

"This isn't the end of my story." Cara said. The battle had stopped around them.

"What the—" he muttered, his paw now hanging at his side.

Cara looked over her shoulder and saw Melissa standing there, her one hand red hot and the other on her back. Melissa was looking at her own hand, amazed.

James's army stopped, stunned at the sight of Melissa.

James staggered to his feet, his eyes shooting daggers as he looked back and forth between them.

"Another human?" he said, confused. Then Cara saw fear wash over him quickly before turning to determination.

"We've got this," Melissa whispered to Cara.

Cara and Melissa each reached down and grabbed swords off the ground, raised them high and ran as fast as they could towards him. He laughed, also grabbing a sword and ran.

Cara swung, but he was ready and blocked the attack. With each hit, her bad shoulder ached in pain and it only got worse. Melissa swung at him too, trying to get his attention away from Cara, but he hit her with such force, she staggered back.

Every attempt Melissa made, his hits grew harder until finally he looked at her and shook his head. He took his free hand, created a blue electric ball and fired it at Melissa, sending her flying back. The armies started battling again; the air filling with the crashing of swords.

Cara watched Melissa fly back, but James wasn't letting up. He swung over and over, each hit getting more intense. She couldn't do this for too much longer. He swung his sword up from the ground and hit with a force she wasn't expecting, and her sword went flying. He laughed.

"Really, Cara. You really aren't much of a challenge anymore, are you? What a shame." He looked at her with eyes that appeared so cold and dead that she shook. He wasn't the animal that she had once trusted.

She slowly backed up. She was weaponless now, and he swaggered over to her. If only she could reach Melissa, but she wasn't getting up.

"I was really looking forward to a good battle. But I guess this is it. I'll just have to defeat you and be done with it."

He raised his sword to chest level and charged. She tried to turn away, but she wasn't quick enough. His sword struck her good shoulder. She screamed out in pain. She dropped to her knees, the sword still in her. Both of her shoulders were hurt now. She knew he had her now. He pulled the blade from her and blood streamed out. She grabbed the injury and held tight. The pain was radiating all over her now.

"This will be pretty sweet after all." He laughed.

He raised the blade again, grinning with evil in his eyes. Cara looked at him again, waiting for the final blow to hit her and her to be done. Just then, a shadow covered her view. Melissa stood above her, her eyes fixed on James.

"You'll have to finish me first," Melissa said, raising her sword.

"This has nothing to do with you," James replied

"She's my friend. This has everything to do with me."

"Don't interfere," he said.

"I have to."

"Oh really. Now you're going to fight her battles for her? Weren't you the one causing all the battles?" James asked.

"Not anymore." Behind her, Cara tried to stand, but the pain that embraced her whole body was making it nearly impossible.

Melissa turned and reached her hand out towards Cara, who took it. She helped her stand. Cara staggered slightly, but got her footing. Melissa grabbed Cara's right hand and looked at Cara. Cara took her left hand and Melissa saw sparks flying. They grew and grew until it was bigger than Cara had ever made on her own.

James watched it grow and finally saw the fear taking over him.

"How—?" he managed, watching it grow bigger than the three of them. He stumbled back to get out of the way as it grew.

"Two humans together? Our magic is even stronger. She doesn't have to have magic to make things happen. She just needs to be here to support me!" Cara yelled.

James's army started backing up and split to let James back up. Cara and Melissa walked towards him and Cara released the electric ball, sending it to the army on the left of James. Most saw it coming and ran as fast as they could. The sphere hit the ground, sending soldiers flying in a cloud of fur and feathers. The soldiers on James's right, knowing what was coming, ran for cover.

In the middle of it all was James, standing by himself. He kept backing up further and further through the trampled field.

Cara started another sphere, ready to send it to James. He was creating his own and sent it to Cara's, trying to break hers, but his bounced off. Even at a distance, Cara could see how scared he was.

Cara and Melissa kept advancing through the field and the sphere got bigger and bigger in Cara's hand. Her army remained close, but no one dared approach them.

"You aren't going to win this," James said, still sending fireballs at them. His were getting bigger too, but they were still no match for theirs.

"You don't understand. Evil doesn't win in the end. Good always triumphs," Cara said.

She raised the ball above her head and threw it over James's head. It flew past him and he turned to watch it go. It went down into the ravine just past the cliff.

Cara watched him, knowing he was terrified, but he held his ground. She shot electric balls one after another at his feet, and he kept backing up. She threw one at his side and he jumped back. His feet were on the edge of the cliff. He wobbled back and forth for a few moments, arms flailing about, trying to get his balance. Cara and Melissa held their breath and then he was gone. Not even a scream came up from him as he fell.

And just like that, James was gone.

Fifty-Two

Cara and Melissa stood stunned.

"He's gone?" Melissa asked, searching Cara's eyes. Cara smiled and gently hugged Melissa. Cara's army cheered and came around them both, embracing them tightly.

"You did it! You saved us!" Cynthia said, helping Cara back away from the cliff edge and towards the middle of the field.

In the distance, the beast let out a shriek and turned to run away. He was quickly shrinking in size and howling in pain. He disappeared behind a tree and they heard a last cry, then silence.

A cheer went up as they hugged and laughed. They were finally free. Turning away from the battlefield, they headed to the lake.

* * *

"We'll miss you," Cynthia said, giving Cara a hug.

"I'll miss you all so much." Cara's heart felt so full. She looked at the faces of those around her. Saying goodbye was never easy, and today was even worse.

"Don't forget us," Cynthia said, grabbing her hand and holding it for a moment.

"I never will." She reached over and gave her another hug and wiped at tears that were now streaming down her face.

"We will never forget what you did for us. Thank you," Terrance said, coming over to her.

She could only nod through the lump that choked her words. She let herself fall into his arms and hugged him.

"We're going back to our town to rebuild. And we're going to make the Dream Writing room even better than before," he said. "You'll have some of the sweetest dreams you've ever had," he assured her.

Melissa gave them a quick wave, and they walked into the lake together. It still was as beautiful as ever and Cara, seeing her friends around her, couldn't believe that she may never see them again. It hurt, but she knew it would be safer if they closed up the passageway.

Cara looked at Cynthia one last time and gave her one last wave. Cynthia had said she would take care of it. Cara and Melissa took a deep breath and plunged into the cool water.

* * *

Cara walked out of the cool water of the pool, dripping. Melissa had helped her through the tunnel, but her body still ached and all she wanted to do was sleep. But she had to get home and let her parents know she was okay.

"Cara, I'm really sorry. And everything that Vanessa has done, too." Melissa said, catching her breath on the pool's edge.

"Thanks. Are we okay now?"

"Definitely."

"What about your mom?" Cara asked.

"I will be okay. You're not the only one that has learnt to stand up for themselves."

"I think she's different now," Cara said, hoping it was true. "When she got here again, her first thought was of you. She wanted to be with you more than anything and was really upset she had been gone this long."

Melissa got up and headed to the door. "Looks like we can still make it for second period." She said, looking at the clock. She turned back to Cara. Cara laughed and followed behind her. Melissa fell in line with Cara and put her arm around her. They walked out of the poolroom together and headed to the outside doors towards their homes.

* * *

Cara arrived back at home and, although her parents were worried about her, because of her letter, they hadn't called the police. They sat around the dining room table and she finally told them everything. Even though she could read the questions all over their faces and the fact they didn't really believe her, they let her tell her story and her mom bandaged her shoulder up.

"Next time you go there, please let one of us come with you, alright?" her mom said.

Cara laughed and gave them a hug. Maybe everything would be okay after all.

Acknowledgements

This book started as a silly idea many years ago for my sons. But as time went on and I saw him struggle with nightmares, it evolved into what it is today. It is a labour of love for my sons and I hope that someday they will read it and love it. Writing a novel has been a dream of mine since I was seven years old. Many times I didn't think I would actually finish writing it. But I'm so thankful to the friends that kept "pushing" me to keep at it and all the brainstorming sessions we had.

I want to thank the people that helped me through the years. To all the people that never stopped believing in me, thank you. To all the ones that encouraged me to keep trying, thank you. To all the ones that helped with editing and formatting, thank you.

To all my family that never stopped believing in me and helping me along the way, thank you. I love you all, and I wouldn't have made it without you.

Author Bio

Kelly Dowswell is a writer from southwestern Ontario. She has a diploma in Journal-Print from Niagara College and has worked in the field doing paginating (page layout) for over a decade for her city's two local newspapers. She's also had several articles and columns published. When she isn't drinking tea and running after her two young sons, she's writing short stories and novels. She has had two short stories published in the anthology Masquerade. This is her debut novel.